Finding God in Tough Times

Books by Kristi Holl

SERIES

The Boarding School Mysteries
Zonderkidz/Faithgirlz

Vanished

Betrayed

Burned

Poisoned

Devotionals
Zonderkidz/Faithgirlz

Finding God in Tough Times

What's a Girl to Do?

Shine On, Girl!

Girlz Rock

Chick Chat

No Boys Allowed

TodaysGirls.com series

4Give & 4Get

Fun E-Farm

Tangled Web

Chat Freak

Carousel Mysteries Mid-Prairie Books

Deadly Disguise

Stage Fright

A Spin Out of Control

"Julie McGregor" Standard Publishing

A Change of Heart

A Tangled Web

Two of a Kind

Trusting in the Dark

SINGLE TITLES

**More Writer's First Aid: Getting the Writing Done
Writer's Institute Publications**

Writer's First Aid • Writer's Institute Publications

For Every Joy That Passes • Royal Fireworks Press

Invisible Alex • Royal Fireworks Press

Danger at Hanging Rock • David C. Cook Publishers

Hidden in the Fog • Atheneum Books for Children

No Strings Attached • Atheneum Books for Children

Patchwork Summer • Atheneum Books for Children

The Haunting of Cabin 13 • Atheneum Books for Children

First Things First • Atheneum Books for Children

OTHER BOOKS

Finding God in Tough Times

Kristi Holl

ZONDERVAN®

ZONDERVAN

Finding God in Tough Times
Copyright © 2013 by Kristi Holl

This title is also available as a Zondervan ebook.
Visit www.zondervan.com/ebooks.

Requests for information should be addressed to:
Zondervan, 3900 Sparks Dr. SE, Grand Rapids, Michigan 49546

Library of Congress Cataloging-in-Publication Data

Holl, Kristi.
     Finding God in tough times
  Holl, Kristi.
        p.   cm.
     ISBN 978-0-310-73180-1 (softcover)
     1. Girls--Prayers and devotions--Juvenile literature. 2. Suffering--
Religious aspects--Christianity--Juvenile literature. I. Title.
BV4860.H6155 2014
248.8'2 — dc23   2013027505

Editor: Kim Childress
Cover design: Cindy Davis
Cover image: Shutterstock
Interior design: Ben Fetterley and Greg Johnson/Textbook Perfect

Fifth printing June 2014 / Printed in the United States of America

2

To Luella Kalvik,
who always helps me find God in the tough times.

Foreword

Everyone has tough times. Everyone. Some worse than others. We live in a broken world, and bad things happen to innocent people. To children. The important thing to know is you are not alone. Christians may know this more than others, that God is with them through the storms. But what if you're a child or a teenager who isn't a Christian, going through horrible situations, like me when I was growing up? Looking back, if someone would have said to me, "You're blessed by your suffering," or "God is perfecting your faith," I'm not sure if that would have done me any good at all. But if someone had said to me, "You're not alone. You have options. There is help. I'm here to help you," I wonder how differently my life would have been. If I had known. If I had been able to see the big picture.

So I was excited and thankful when Kristi Holl shared with me her idea for this book. We wanted to help others. Other kids. Maybe you. To let you know that you are not alone. God is with you, always, and there is help available if you need it. And maybe, just maybe, you can find good in your hardship, or perhaps help others in need, whether now or in the future. And perhaps you can experience the love of God and Jesus Christ in your life, and discover how you can share his love with another person who may be hurting. For now, just know, God is with you.

–Kim Childress, Editor

Introduction

Do you envy friends and classmates who have what you think of as "normal," everyday problems? They worry about boys ("Does he like me?"). They obsess about body image ("Do these jeans make me look fat?"). They moan over bad hair days ("Cover my head with a sack!"). They complain about having no money ("I'll die if I don't get that CD!"). You'd give anything to have normal worries.

To be honest, you don't even know what *normal* is!

Why? There can be many reasons. You might live with parents who are fighting, divorcing, dating, or remarrying. You may be adjusting to stepparents or step-siblings. You might have a friend on drugs. In your loneliness, you may have met someone online, but your parents worry about online safety. Maybe your dad lost his job—and you've lost your home. And sadly, you may be the victim of some kind of abuse.

Although you may try to hide it, you might feel afraid, depressed, lonely, and angry. But no matter what the problem is—or how you feel—nothing is too small to take to God or too big for God to handle.

You probably have more questions than answers at times like these.

- Is God there?
- Does He care about what you're going through?

- Can He help you?
- *Will* He help you?

The answer to each of those questions is Yes! Not maybe. Not "I hope so." But a loud yes!

So how do you find God in the tough times? The following 90 devotionals will help you do that.

Believe it or not, security and self-worth can't be found in having pleasant circumstances. We love pleasant circumstances, and we should be grateful for them! They're wonderful! But you can find a *false* sense of security and self-worth in having things go your way. Then when problems hit (as they do for everyone) that security will crumble. You can—you *must*—learn to find your security in Christ alone. You can, even in tough times.

The 90 devotions cover a variety of topics and problems. If you want to find other devotions on a particular subject, look at the bottom of that page. There you will find the words "Indexed under" and one or more topics. Simply flip to the index at the back of the book, look up that topic in the alphabetical listing, and find more help on that subject.

May God bless you in the study of his Word, and may you feel God's overwhelming love for you.

Devotion #1

"For God has not given us a spirit of fear and timidity, but of power, love, and self-discipline."

(2 Timothy 1:7 NLT)

Fighting Fear God's Way

Grace took a deep breath and steadied her shaking knees. She would have given anything not to walk into another new school. But with Dad in the Air Force, her family moved every year. No matter how many times she started over at a new school, she always found it terrifying: the curious eyes staring at her, teachers making her introduce herself to the class, getting lost, sitting alone in the lunch room ...

Students jostled Grace as she walked up the school steps to the front door. She felt invisible as she pushed through the crowd. *No one will like me*, she thought. *I'll never have friends.* She headed down the hallway to her locker, then stopped ... confused. Someone ran into her. Afraid to ask for directions, Grace flowed with the crowd until she spotted a restroom. She dashed inside, headed for a stall, and locked the door.

Tears welled up in her eyes, and with a shaking hand, Grace brushed them aside. *Stop this*, she told herself. She closed her eyes, said a quick prayer for help, and then repeated the verse Mom had encouraged her to memorize. "God hasn't given me a spirit of fear," Grace whispered. "He gave me power and love and a well-balanced mind."

Pulling her shoulders back, Grace took several deep breaths before leaving the restroom. She walked up to two girls, smiled brightly, and asked directions to the sixth-grade lockers.

"Are you new?" the tall one asked, smiling back. "Come on. We'll show you."

Grace walked down the hall between the girls and prayed, *Thank you, God!*

More to Explore: "God is love. Whoever lives in love lives in God, and God in them . . . There is no fear in love." (1 John 4:16, 18)

Connecting to God: "Dear God, sometimes I'm so afraid of going into new situations and meeting new people. When I'm afraid, help me remember that you're with me. I trust you to take care of me. Amen."

Journal Prompt: How can you prepare, with God's help, for some event that you fear?

Take Action: Fear urges you to believe in what you see as your outward circumstances and doubt the unseen — God and His promises. When sneaky little lies pop into your mind, speak up and tell the truth — out loud!

Lie: *Nobody loves you.*
TRUTH: God loves me "with an everlasting love." (Jeremiah 31:3)

Lie: *You're all alone.*
TRUTH: God is "with [me] and will watch over [me] wherever [I] go!" (Genesis 28:15)

Lie: *You're too afraid to do this.*
TRUTH: "I can do all this through [Christ] who gives me strength!" (Philippians 4:13)

Real-girl Confession: "I have panic attacks and throw up every time someone asks me how I feel about starting a new school."

Indexed under: fear, loneliness

Devotion #2

"Speaking the truth in love, [we] may grow up in all things."

(Ephesians 4:14 – 15 NKJV)

Caught in the Middle

Sophia called, "Hi, I'm home!" when she walked into the house on Sunday night, but she hoped Mom didn't hear her. As usual, she tried slipping upstairs to her room without being seen, but Mom popped out of the kitchen.

"Hey, wait a minute!" Mom called. "How was your weekend with Dad and what's-her-name?"

Sophia sighed. She dreaded these Sunday night cross-examinations. They always followed a weekend visit with Dad and his new wife.

Mom cornered her and began grilling. "Did you go to church today? And did you remind him about the late support check? We can't buy groceries this week without it."

Sophia stared at the floor. Sometimes she felt like a messenger boy. Other times she felt like a spy.

Mom stood with hands on her hips. "I saw the fancy car they brought you home in. How much did *that* cost?"

"How would I know that?" Sophia asked, trying hard to sound reasonable.

"You could find out if you wanted to."

Sophia threw her hands in the air. "Am I supposed to snoop

through Dad's desk?" She ran to the top of the stairs and turned back. "Can't you be nice? Dad never asks nosy questions about *you!*" She ran down the hall to her room and slammed the door.

One day, Sophia's Sunday school teacher asked about her life. For a change, Sophia opened up — about how she hated being caught in the middle and how upsetting it was. Her teacher suggested that Sophia be kind, but honest, with her mom. "Tell her how you feel," her teacher encouraged her, "but speak the truth in love, as the Bible says."

After the next visitation weekend, Sophia was ready. Mom asked question after question about how Dad lived his life and spent his money. Sophia smiled and took a deep breath.

"Mom," she said, "the divorce is between you and Dad. If you need to talk to him, please do it directly." She hugged her mom. "I love you, and I love Dad too. But I don't want to be caught in the middle anymore."

Mom looked a bit embarrassed. "I don't need you to tell me what to do."

"I'm not," Sophia said. "I guess I'm saying what I don't want to do. I don't want to carry your messages to Dad anymore."

Over the next few weeks, Sophia had to mention her decision a couple more times. "I'm just a kid. I really want you and Dad to talk to each other instead of pass messages through me."

"You're right," Mom finally said one day. "It's my job to communicate my questions directly. From now on, I will."

"Thanks, Mom."

More to Explore: "We can say with confidence and a clear conscience that we have lived with a God-given holiness and sincerity in all our dealings." (2 Corinthians 1:12 NLT)

Connecting to God: "Dear Lord, it's hard being caught in the middle of people's problems. Give me courage to speak the truth in love and let them resolve their own issues. Please keep my heart at peace. Amen."

Journal Prompt: Learning new behaviors takes time. Controlling your emotions so you can speak up respectfully can take a while to learn. What can you do when you feel like giving up?

Take Action: QUIZ: Underline the responses that "speak the truth in love."

"How could you make such a stupid mistake?"

"I believe your answer is wrong, but we don't have to agree on everything."

"I don't speak to you in that tone, so please show me the same respect."

"You probably lost the race because you're so fat."

"Those pink jeans are pretty, but I think I like the black ones better."

"I hate you for saying that to me!"

"Your story needs some more work to make the ending stronger."

Real-girl Confession: "I'm supposed to tell my dad stuff like, 'Mom needs money — why aren't we getting any?'"

Indexed under: divorce, honesty, stepfamilies, resentment

Devotion #3

"Even if my father and mother abandon me, the LORD will hold me close."

(Psalm 27:10 NLT)

Feeling Forgotten

Megan grabbed the music for her solo, glanced again at the clock, and hurried after Mom to the car. "Don't worry," Mom said. "Dad's just running late. He probably plans to meet us at the school."

I don't believe that any more than you do, Megan thought, buckling her seat belt. "He hardly ever shows up for anything important to me, including my last birthday party," she said aloud. Megan slumped down in the seat and stared out the window. "I bet Dad's in some bar downtown."

Even though it hurt, it might actually be better if he missed her music program. Megan shuddered at the memory of last year's championship volleyball game. They'd had to stop the game when Dad fell off the end of the bleachers and got hurt. Megan squirmed at the memory of her teammates' snickers and pitying looks.

As Megan's mom pulled into the school parking lot, her cell phone rang. She glanced at the caller ID. "It's your dad," she said. The call lasted less than a minute. A moment later, looking straight ahead, Mom said in a grim voice, "Someone gave your dad an expensive ticket for a baseball game tonight. He's going with some friends."

Megan knew without asking that it was a drinking buddy. "I don't care," she muttered, feeling the familiar stab of pain. How could Dad's friends and his drinking be more important than her recital? Megan knew she'd never understand, even if she lived to be a hundred.

Mom reached over and gripped Megan's hand. "I'm so sorry, honey. Let's pray before you go in. 'Dear Lord, help Megan remember that her heavenly Father is always with her, always loving her, always proud of her, and always thinking of her. Amen.'"

"Thanks, Mom." Megan's heart felt a new warmth. She walked inside the auditorium to sing her solo, knowing God the Father's loving presence is with her at all times.

More to Explore: "Never! Can a mother forget her nursing child? Can she feel no love for the child she has borne? But even if that were possible, I [God] would not forget you! See, I have written your name on the palms of my hands." (Isaiah 49:15 – 16 NLT)

Connecting to God: "Dear God, sometimes I feel forgotten and abandoned. Please hold me close. Thank you that you never forget me and always love me. And thank you for loving my dad too. Help him to find your love. Amen."

Journal Prompt: Pretend you are writing to a teacher, counselor, or a friend's parent. Tell them what it feels like to live with someone who drinks too much.

Take Action: If you have a parent who drinks too much, you can't fix it or make your parent stop. You can take better care of yourself though. Write the following "six Cs" on a card. When you're scared or don't know what to do, read this out loud.

Remember the Six Cs:

I didn't **C**ause the drinking.

I can't **C**ure the drinking.

I can't **C**ontrol the drinking.

I can take better **C**are of myself.

I can **C**ommunicate with God in prayer.

I can make healthy **C**hoices.

(from National Association for Children of Alcoholics at http://www.nacoa.org/)

Real-girl Confession: "Is it my fault Dad drinks too much? Will I become an alcoholic too?"

Indexed under: abandonment, alcoholism, sadness

Devotion #4

"For the wages of sin is death, but the free gift of God is eternal life through Christ Jesus our Lord."

(Romans 6:23 NLT)

Following Jesus — or Faking It?

Laney loved church camp. For a whole week, she got to bunk in a cabin with other girls her age plus a student counselor. They spent their days swimming, canoeing, making crafts, and attending sing-alongs, bonfires, and cookouts.

The only thing Laney wished she could skip was the evening Bible study with their counselor. Laney liked the peppy sing-along Jesus songs, with all the stomping and clapping. But the Bible study was too long, and the counselor asked too many personal questions.

"Grab your Bibles and gather in the middle here," their counselor, Gabby, called. "Tonight's subject is prayer."

"Oh, great," Laney muttered, pulling her Bible from the cubby beside her cot.

"What's the matter?" her friend Mya asked.

"Nothing." Laney didn't want to talk about prayer. Prayer didn't really work. At least it didn't help *her*. The counselor talked about Jesus like he was her best friend. Gabby called it a "personal relationship," but it didn't feel like that to Laney. She knew a lot of stories *about* Jesus, but he didn't feel like a friend. That whole idea seemed fakey.

After the study on the Lord's Prayer, Gabby said they would go around the circle. Each girl would pray about anything on her mind.

Laney rolled her eyes at Mya. She wished she could get up and leave. When it was her turn, Laney sat in silence. She honestly couldn't think of anything to say.

Gabby smiled. "It's okay. Many girls are shy about praying in a group. Just give it a try."

Laney hunched her shoulders.

Gabby touched Laney's hand. "Just pretend you're at home, and pray like you would normally."

Laney shrugged. "I don't really pray at home. It doesn't seem to change anything."

"Oh. Well, maybe we can talk about that later," Gabby said. "For now, I'll close in prayer."

After the girls were zipped into their sleeping bags, Gabby came to Laney's bunk. "Laney, can I ask you something?" Gabby said.

Laney took a deep breath. "I guess so."

"Can you tell me how old you were when you asked Jesus to come into your life?"

"What do you mean?"

"I'm just asking at what point you chose to be a follower of Jesus."

Laney wriggled in her sleeping bag, feeling very uncomfortable, like she was going to flunk a test or something. "Well, I was baptized when I was a baby," she said, "and I go to church every week."

"Those are good things," Gabby assured her. "Jesus is certainly with the babies and small children—with all children. But was there ever a point when you consciously turned to God? When you asked Jesus to come into your heart? It's a choice you have to make yourself when you're old enough to choose."

"Is that when Jesus feels like your friend?" Laney asked.

"That's when it starts," Gabby said. "The more time you spend with him, the closer you are. It's a little like spending time with Mya—the more time you spend together, the more you talk to each other, the better friends you are."

"Oh." Laney bit her lower lip. "Thank you for explaining that."

That night in bed after lights-out, Laney thought about Gabby's words. Had she been feeling lonely and fakey all this time because she really wasn't a believer? It made sense that she couldn't choose to follow Jesus as a baby, but she didn't remember making a choice when she was older either.

Well, she wasn't going to let another day go by without choosing Jesus. In the quiet of the dark cabin, she listened to the chorus of crickets and bullfrogs. Then Laney invited Jesus into her heart. Peace filled her as she thought about her new friend—and she slipped into a deep sleep.

More to Explore: "For everyone has sinned; we all fall short of God's glorious standard." (Romans 3:23 NLT)

Connecting to God: "Dear God, I know Jesus rose from the dead for my sins. I accept Jesus into my heart as my Savior. Help me to experience your love and live how you want me to live. Amen."

Journal Prompt: Write about the time you decided to become a follower of Jesus.

Take Action: Have you heard of the Four Spiritual Laws?

> **Law #1** God loves you and offers a wonderful plan for your life. (John 10:10)

Law #2 Man is sinful and separated from God so he can't experience God's love or good plan. (Romans 6:23)

Law #3 Jesus is God's only plan for man's sin. Through Jesus you can know God's love. (John 1:12)

Law #4 We must individually receive Jesus Christ as Savior and Lord; then we can know and experience God's love and plan for our lives. (Ephesians 2:8 – 9)

Real-girl Confession: "I feel like a fake at church."

Indexed under: distant from God, loneliness, salvation

Devotion #5

"You should keep a clear mind in every situation."

(2 Timothy 4:5 NLT)

You're Such a Baby!

Emily kicked at the crunchy fallen leaves on the sidewalk as she headed to school. She'd be glad when Friday was over. She didn't feel ready for her math test, and she dreaded giving a speech on her favorite president of the United States. "I wish today was over," she muttered.

Chloe's eyes sparkled. "Let's just skip school today. Come to my house!" She giggled and grabbed Emily's arm. "Mom already left for work, and I've got a new DVD you just have to see!" Chloe turned and started back down the sidewalk in the direction of her house.

After a few steps, Emily pulled her arm loose. "Very funny," she said, "but if we don't hurry, we'll miss the school bus."

"Hey, I wasn't kidding! Let's skip."

For a brief moment, Emily imagined a day free of math tests and speeches. It sounded heavenly. Then she shook her head. "You know we can't do that."

Chloe rolled her eyes. "You're such a baby."

Emily's face grew hot. Chloe often wanted to do things that made Emily uncomfortable. Still, for some reason, obeying the rules *did* make Emily feel like a baby sometimes.

Chloe trudged toward the bus stop. "I don't know why I even hang out with you. I'll invite Georgia to sleep over tonight instead."

"Thanks a lot," Emily mumbled, shoulders slumped. Now she was a baby nobody wanted!

Then Emily remembered something her Sunday school teacher had said—about how precious Emily was to God and how much he loved her. In fact, Jesus was her best friend, and he always wanted her around.

Emily stood up straight. "I'm not a baby," she said, "and I don't think skipping school is so grown up." *And,* she thought, *what Chloe says about me doesn't count. I'm a child of God, and that's all that matters.*

More to Explore: "Don't copy the behavior and customs of this world, but let God transform you into a new person by changing the way you think. Then you will learn to know God's will for you, which is good and pleasing and perfect." (Romans 12:2 NLT)

Connecting to God: "Dear Lord, sometimes the world isn't a friendly place. People say hurtful things about me that just aren't true. Thank you for telling me the truth that sets me free. Amen."

Journal Prompt: It's hard to make good choices when you're too upset to think calmly. How can you put a brake on runaway feelings?

Take Action: Sometimes friends might pressure you to do what is wrong. What can you say?

A. "I'm not interested in doing that. It's just not me."

B. "I'm not comfortable doing that, and I have to do what's right for me."

C. "I have other things I'd rather do with my time [or money]."

D. For the really brave with a friend who might listen ... "The Bible says that's wrong. I want to keep you for a friend, but I want to please God even more."

Real-girl Confession: "I'm scared to stand up to my friend. Should I just get new friends?"

Indexed under: peer pressure, temptation

Devotion #6

"No good is going to come from that crowd; they spend all their time cooking up gossip against those who mind their own business."

(Psalm 35:20 MSG)

Wagging Tongues

Courtney walked past the lunch line acting like she didn't even want any pizza. It was her favorite meal, but she'd packed her healthful — and cheaper — lunch. She would do it until Dad found another job. It wasn't Dad's fault he was out of work; the whole company went out of business. Dad hunted for a new job every day.

At the end of the lunch line, Courtney stopped to grab a paper napkin. Her hand froze when she heard her name.

"Courtney always thought she was so *hot*." It was her friend, Brooke. "Guess where I saw her Saturday? It wasn't the Gap."

"Where was she?" Vanessa asked.

"Goodwill!" Brooke laughed. "You know — where you buy donated junk."

Courtney felt her face flush, and her hand shook as she grabbed the napkins. There was nothing wrong with Goodwill, but she hadn't been shopping there. She had gone to Walmart for some new jeans because her old ones with the designer label were too short now. Why was Brooke lying? They were friends!

As Courtney turned to go to her table, she heard Brooke

say, "Courtney's dad got fired, you know. I heard he stole money from the company."

"Really?" Vanessa asked. "Is he going to jail?"

"He's probably there already."

Near tears, Courtney hurried to her table. Her stomach hurt too much now to eat, so she threw her lunch in the trash and went to the restroom. She'd always known Brooke liked to gossip—Courtney used to listen to her just like Vanessa was doing now. *Not anymore though*, Courtney thought. She'd had no idea how much gossip could hurt.

At least Courtney had learned one thing. When times were hard, she needed friends—the *real* kind. Not the kind who gossiped behind her back. *Courtney, it's time to forgive them—and then find some new friends*, she heard God's voice clearly in her spirit.

More to Explore: "All day long you plot destruction. Your tongue cuts like a sharp razor; you're an expert at telling lies." (Psalm 52:2 NLT)

Connecting to God: "Dear God, I feel hurt when people talk about me, especially when they don't tell the truth. I don't want to be a bitter person. Help me to forgive them and to treat others the way I want to be treated. Amen."

Journal Prompt: Gossip hurts. How do you handle it when someone hurts you, but they do not seem to be sorry?

Take Action: Take steps to stop gossip in your circle. Be part of the solution instead of the problem. Before passing along information about another person, ask yourself these questions:

    A. Is it true?

    B. Is it kind?

    C. Is it necessary to pass this information along?

If you answer "no" to any of those questions, zip your lip. Stop gossip by not engaging in it.

Real-girl Confession: "My best friend's mad at me, so she's telling everyone my worst secrets!"

Indexed under: friendship, gossip, job loss

Devotion #7

"Therefore I tell you, do not worry about your life, what you will eat or drink; or about your body, what you will wear. Is not life more than food, and the body more than clothes?"

(Matthew 6:25)

God *Will* Provide!

Christina sat at the kitchen table, pretending to do her homework. She was unable to concentrate on her work as she watched Mom shuffle bills back and forth from one pile to another. It made Christina's stomach churn.

Since the divorce, money was tight. Christina's family hadn't lost their house—yet. There was no money for eating out anymore, though. Not even pizza! Christina missed the things they used to buy, but that was nothing compared to her nightmares about being kicked out of their house.

"Is your homework done?" Mom asked.

Christina's hand jerked. "No, not yet."

"I'm not done either." Mom gave a half smile. "I keep trying to make a stretched-out dollar stretch even more."

Christina's voice was low. "I thought Dad sends child support payments."

"Yes, he does," Mom said, "and it's a real help. But sometimes his payments are late, so we need to live on what I make."

Christina frowned. "Can we do that?"

"Yes, by using a budget," Mom explained. "It helps take the worry out of finances."

Christina frowned. "What's a budget?"

"A spending plan," Mom said. "You give some of your income back to God, you save some for emergencies, and you trust God to make the rest cover your needs. God is the one who provides everything in the first place, but we need to be wise and not squander."

They talked about ways Christina and her brothers could help save money at home. "Turning off the lights and TV when they're not in use," Mom said, "will help lower the electric bill."

"And we can try not to waste food," Christina said, "by putting leftovers in the fridge for the next day."

Mom nodded. Soon they had a list of ten things they could do as a family to cut expenses. They would do their part. Then Christina would trust God to do his part. And she would learn to be content with what God provided.

More to Explore: "Keep your lives free from the love of money and be content with what you have, because God has said, 'Never will I leave you; never will I forsake you.'" (Hebrews 13:5)

Connecting to God: "Dear God, I worry about having enough money. Help me remember that you provide all we need and to be thankful for what I have. Amen."

Journal Prompt: It's challenging to trust someone you can't actually see with your eyes. How can I build trust in God to take care of me?

Take Action: Want a fun (and *smart*) way to budget your money? Use four little banks, boxes, or containers. Label each bank with the way you'll use the money: SAVE, SPEND, INVEST, and GIVE.

A spending bank is for money to be used soon on everyday things, like candy or gum.

A saving bank is for money to be used later on larger items, like a shirt or CD.

An investing bank is for money that will be used a year or more from now, like for a bike or toward college.

A giving bank is for gifts to help others.

Decorate each bank with stickers, photographs, or magazine clippings, showing how the money will be used. Wisely use the money God provides.

Real-girl Confession: "I worry about money all the time. I don't like to tell Mom when I run out of lunch money."

Indexed under: divorce, finances, worry

Devotion #8

"Love . . . always looks for the best."

(1 Corinthians 13:7 MSG)

No More Macaroni!

Isabella was angry when her mom took a job working the night shift at the hospital. Now her mom left for work before Isabella got home from school, and her shift ended long after Isabella was in bed. Isabella used to love supper time, when Mom and Dad asked about her day while they ate Mom's homemade pizza or lasagna.

But now? Every night, Dad called, "Izzy, supper's ready!" It was always the same: hot dogs or macaroni-and-cheese, eaten on snack trays in front of the evening newscast. Then Isabella did homework and went to bed. As the weeks passed, Isabella grew more and more resentful. *Mom doesn't care about me, or she wouldn't work nights,* she thought. *And Dad doesn't care about me or he'd fix better meals and talk to me.*

Then one day, Isabella's Sunday school teacher talked to the class about love. "One way to love someone, according to First Corinthians 13:7, is to choose to believe the best about him or her." He grinned at the class. "Try that with your friends and family instead of being mad at them. They'll feel better if you do—and so will you."

Isabella decided it was worth a try. *Believe the best about Mom,* she told herself. Well, Mom is working hard for the family and probably lonely for them at night too. *Believe the best about Dad too*, she told herself. Well, Dad really can't cook, but he tries. Isabella decided to try something to make things better.

After school, she went to the library to check out some kids' cookbooks that showed how to make simple meals. She asked Dad to learn a few new recipes with her. He agreed, and they enjoyed talking—and laughing—while they cooked. Two nights that week the meal turned out so good that they saved some as a treat for Mom when she got home.

The following Sunday, Isabella told her Sunday school teacher how things had changed at home when she followed his advice. "It was *God's* advice," he said, patting her shoulder, "and I'm glad you tried it." He sat down next to her. "We can't control many of the circumstances in our lives, but God's ways help us quiet our upset emotions. Believing the best about every person is a great place to start."

"And cooking with Dad is actually fun," Isabella said. "Something bad turned into something good!"

More to Explore: "Think about things that are excellent and worthy of praise." (Philippians 4:8 NLT)

Connecting to God: "Dear God, sometimes I get so mad when people do things I don't like. Help me to understand them better and believe the best about them. Amen."

Journal Prompt: Are my angry feelings covering up other true feelings? When I feel angry, am I hurt or afraid?

Take Action: It's important to give people "the benefit of the doubt." If their behavior can be taken two different ways, choose the kind explanation. However, believing the best about someone does *not* mean being in denial about bad behavior. If someone screams nasty insults at you, it doesn't help anyone to tell yourself, "He's so kind." So ... what *truthful* things can you say about someone in a situation where their behavior is clearly negative?

"He's probably doing the best he can."

"She might have big problems I know nothing about."

"He's probably hurting inside, and hurting people hurt other people."

Real-girl Confession: "Why do parents make big family decisions without even asking their kids how they feel?"

Indexed under: abandonment, anger, resentment

Devotion #9

"My only aim is to finish the race and complete the task the Lord Jesus has given me — the task of testifying to the good news of God's grace."

(Acts 20:24 TNIV)

The Finish Line

Kristen accepted a summer job helping her neighbor who owned a dog kennel. He needed helpers to walk and feed the dogs, plus do some cleanup. Kristen was eager to begin. The only other summer job available for twelve-year-old girls was weekend babysitting. She had prayed hard for a different job. Working with dogs — especially newborn puppies — sounded like heaven to Kristen. She'd be getting paid for playing with puppies and taking dogs for walks. She thanked God many times for this job.

However, Kristen soon learned that working in a dog kennel was hard — and often stinky — work. Very little of her time was spent walking dogs or playing with puppies. Most of her days were spent cleaning dirty kennels. The smell sometimes made her gag. And all that barking! She thought she might go deaf by the end of the summer. When it was time to feed the dogs, the frenzied barking made her ears ring. And some of the dogs scared her. She understood that many of them were frightened about being away from home, but they snarled and bared their teeth at her when she tried to comfort them.

Kristen wanted to quit her job every time her alarm went off in the morning. But she remembered praying for her job and agreeing to help out for the summer. Determined to finish the job God had given her, she dragged herself out of bed. She put on her oldest jeans, tied back her long hair, and headed to the kennel. She stuck it out and finished the summer. Her neighbor said she was the best young worker he'd ever had ... and surprised her with an end-of-season bonus check!

More to Explore: "I have fought the good fight, I have finished the race, I have kept the faith." (2 Timothy 4:7 TNIV)

Connecting to God: "Dear God, I want to be strong and finish the plan you've laid out for my life. Sometimes, the work seems too hard and I want to quit. Help me remember to ask you every day for the energy I need to keep going. Amen."

Journal Prompt: What is your ideal job and why? Are you doing anything to pursue your dream? If not, what can you do now to change that?

Take Action: Sometimes, the things you want cost more money than you have. What can you do to earn some extra money? Here are a few ideas to get you started:

Home projects Ask your parents if you can help with any big projects around the house, such as cleaning or organizing the garage or basement. Ask your parents about jobs they can't find time to do.

Yard work for neighbors Offer your services for grass cutting, snow shoveling, leaf raking, weed pulling, and lawn watering.

Wash cars With your parents' permission, use your garden hose and driveway for a car wash.

Babysit little kids Take a class or read books about babysitting.

Pet service While people are on vacation, care for their pets. It can be done at their home or yours, if your parents are OK with it.

Real-girl Confession: "Why is starting something so much easier than finishing it?"

Indexed under: perseverance

Devotion #10

"Do not nurse hatred in your heart for any of your relatives."

(Leviticus 19:17 NLT)

Reaching My Boiling Point!

Mia's family moved in with her grandfather while their new house was being built, and Mia couldn't wait for it to be finished. "I can't stand Grandpa," she muttered to herself. "He makes me absolutely sick!"

When Grandpa was asleep, Mia talked to Mom. "Grandpa is so mean! He's ruining my life. He criticizes my clothes, he told my friend her hair looks like *weeds*, and he makes fun of my music." She stomped up and down the living room. "And he says *I* have bad manners! Can't we go to a motel?" she begged.

Mom sighed. "You know we can't afford a motel right now. All our money is going into the new house." She lowered her voice. "I know he's cranky, but try to be patient."

"Cranky?" Mia cried. "*Cranky*? He's a monster, and I hate him!"

That night Mia had a hard time falling asleep. The next morning, Grandpa complained when he had to wait his turn for the bathroom. He pounded on the door and yelled until Mia opened the door.

"That's it!" Mia exploded. "I hate you! I'd rather camp out under a bridge than live here!"

Grandpa's mouth dropped open, but no words came out. He shuffled down the hallway to his bedroom and closed the door. Mia turned and saw her mother standing there.

Mia wanted to run away and hide. She was horrified at what had come out of her mouth. For weeks she'd been able to keep the hatred bottled up. "I'm sorry," she said to her mom. "Something inside me just exploded."

Mom nodded. "It was bound to happen, the way you were nursing such disgust for your grandpa. You can't feed hatred in your heart without expecting it to come out sooner or later."

Mia sighed. "I guess I'd better try to make it right with him," Mia said. *God, please help me do this,* she prayed. *Please take away the resentment I feel, and give me your love for Grandpa instead.*

It took a while for Mia and Grandpa's relationship to heal. Mia asked forgiveness for her angry outburst, even though she still disliked some things Grandpa did. Then she took Mom's advice and chose to stop complaining about him to family and friends. This helped shrink the hate in her heart until it finally disappeared.

Mia still needed to bite her tongue sometimes when Grandpa said annoying things. God helped her see that Grandpa had his own adjustments, sharing his house with three people when he was used to living alone. On the day they moved into their new house, Mia was shocked at how God had changed her feelings.

"I'm going to miss you!" she said, giving Grandpa a hug. And she honestly meant it.

More to Explore: "People may cover their hatred with pleasant words, but they're deceiving you. They pretend to be kind, but don't believe them. Their hearts are full of many evils. While their hatred may be concealed by trickery, they're wrongdoing will be exposed in public." (Proverbs 26:24 – 26 NLT)

Connecting to God: "Dear God, you know how hateful and angry I get when family members do things that annoy me. Please replace the hate in my heart with your love. Help me to forgive them and find something positive about them to like. Amen."

Journal Prompt: What steps can you take before you even get out of bed in the morning to have a better day?

Take Action: To get along with grandparents, treat them the way you treat your friends.

> You treat your friends with patience, even when they (or you) are in a bad mood.
>
> You listen to what your friends have to say, even if you don't agree.
>
> You give your friends the benefit of the doubt, most of the time anyway.
>
> You smile at your friends and ask them about their lives.
>
> You compliment your friends and help them feel supported.
>
> If you treat your *grandparents* like your *friends*, your heart will overflow with love for them.

Real-girl Confession: "Living here feels like a prison!"

Indexed under: anger, complaining, resentment

Devotion #11

"Make every effort to live in peace with everyone . . . and see to it that no bitter root grows up to cause trouble."

(Hebrews 12:14–15)

I Can't Stand This Anymore!

Madison trudged down the hallway in her family's apartment and threw her school bag across her bedroom floor. Except it wasn't *her* bedroom anymore. Her six-year-old stepsister, Hannah, now shared it. Madison hated the lack of privacy. She would never get used to a total stranger watching her undress or listening to her phone conversations. And the mess! Madison gritted her teeth, folded up Hannah's Twister game, and angrily swept some glittery beads off her desk.

"You're home!" Hannah cried, bouncing into the bedroom. "Wanna play Twister?"

"No! And stop trashing my room!"

"It's *my* room now too." Hannah stuck out her tongue. "You're mean." She ran out of the room and shouted, "Daddy!"

Madison fell back on her bed and groaned. This dumb family was never going to "blend." It had been three months, and she still felt like they were strangers. Madison just wanted them to go away.

A minute later there was a knock at her door. "Mind if I come in?" Mom asked.

Madison flung one arm over her eyes and sighed. "I can't stand this anymore."

Mom sat on the bed and stroked Madison's arm. "I know you can't imagine us ever feeling like a family, but we will. It just takes time. Meanwhile, try to be patient with Hannah."

Madison sat up. "I can't! I've tried, but I can't!"

"No, you can't," Mom agreed. "You'll have to ask God for help every day. I do."

"Really? You?"

"Sure. I find it hard too. But when you pray, you open a door for God to work. Otherwise, it's very easy for bitterness and resentment to take over." Mom hugged Madison hard. "Hang in there. It *will* get better. I believe God is working. You'll see."

"I hope you're right." Madison smiled and reached for the Twister game. "Guess I'll go find Hannah."

More to Explore: "How wonderful and pleasant it is when brothers live together in harmony!" (Psalm 133:1 NLT)

Connecting to God: "Dear Lord, sometimes I feel I can't go on, like I'm going to explode. I try hard to be patient and forgive, but I really need your help! Please give me patience with those around me. Amen."

Journal Prompt: Martin Luther King Jr. said, "We may all have come on different ships, but we're in the same boat now." How does that apply to your family? Does it change how you might feel toward extended family members?

Take Action: *Tips for bonding with a stepsibling*:

Make a scrapbook to showcase the memories you are making.

Watch a funny movie together, either at home or at the theater.

Play an old-fashioned backyard game, like croquet or badminton.

Just remember: Don't sweat the small stuff! Too often we make a big deal out of nothing.

Real-girl Confession: "Why can't everybody just *leave me alone*?"

Indexed under: resentment, stepfamilies

Devotion #12

"In my distress I cried out to the LORD; yes, I cried to my God for help ... My cry reached his ears."

(2 Samuel 22:7 NLT)

A Very Tough Decision

Claire had been taken to the emergency room four times during the past year. Each time, she lied about her injuries. She claimed her broken arm happened when she fell out of a tree. She insisted her cracked rib came from playing a neighborhood football game. And the gash in her head was from diving into the pool—or so she said.

This time, she blamed her black eye on a baseball. The doctor in charge examined her eye, said very little, and then put an ice pack back on it.

"Can I go now?" Claire asked. "Mom's waiting for me."

"Not yet." He flipped through her chart, frowning. "First, I need to know how you really got hurt this time. I also wonder about the injuries listed in your file from the past year. Please, tell me what's going on. I want to help you."

Heart pounding, Claire stared at the floor. She couldn't tell! She'd promised. Anyway, Dad was really sorry every time. He just kept losing his temper. Each time, he promised it would be the last time. How could she possibly report him? She still loved him, but she had to admit that she also really feared him.

"If you keep protecting this person," the doctor said softly, "it will keep happening. I want to help you. Someone in your life also really needs help. Covering up for him—or her—isn't really helping."

Claire glanced at the kind doctor, and a tear slipped down her cheek.

The doctor took her hand and squeezed it. "Claire, I know this is scary. I've learned in my life that God will help me when I need courage. He will help you be brave too. Just ask him."

Claire took a deep breath and finally nodded. *God, please help me do this*, she prayed. Then, bit by bit, she told the doctor about her experiences.

More to Explore: "A hot-tempered person must pay the penalty." (Proverbs 19:19)

Connecting to God: "Dear Lord, you know what's happening in my home and how afraid I am to tell someone about it. Please give me the courage to reach out so my family can get the help we need. Guide my family, and show me what to do. Amen."

Journal Prompt: How does your body feel when you are afraid? Your head? Your stomach? Your back?

Take Action:

If the abuse is happening *right now*, dial 9-1-1 for immediate police protection.

If the abuse has already happened (to you, a sibling, or a friend), report it to:

your pastor or Sunday school teacher

a child abuse or domestic violence hotline

a teacher or counselor at school
a trusted neighbor or family friend
a grandparent or a friend's parent
a favorite aunt or other relative
the police department or child protective services

Real-girl Confession: "I thought I deserved every punch I got, so I kept it a secret."

Indexed under: abuse/physical, anger, fear, honesty, secrets

Devotion #13

"Happy are those who reject the advice of evil people, who do not follow the example of sinners."

(Psalm 1:1 GNT)

Troublemaking Friends

Julia had been best friends with Kimberly since first grade, ever since Julia's family moved in next door. Lately, though, something had changed. Kimberly smarted off to teachers now, and she often lied to her parents about where she was going after school. Julia also noticed that Kimberly enjoyed stirring up trouble by spreading rumors.

Although Julia hated to admit it, lately she was embarrassed to hang out with Kimberly. The dirty language made Julia blush, and Kimberly just laughed when Julia asked her to stop. The final straw happened one morning before school, when Kimberly took something that didn't belong to her. Because Julia was with her, the teacher assumed Julia was guilty too, and so both girls got detention. Kimberly didn't seem to mind detention at all. In fact, she almost acted proud of it. But Julia hated it, and she couldn't stand the disappointed look in her teacher's eyes.

Julia didn't want to snitch on Kimberly. After all, they'd been friends for five years. Julia couldn't imagine not hanging out with Kimberly, or running back and forth between their houses. So Julia kept quiet and stayed friends with Kimberly.

But she knew she'd have to make a choice soon. Her reputation at school had been damaged, and Kimberly's gossip had hurt some of her other friends.

One day Julia talked to Kimberly as they walked home from school. She explained her feelings about Kimberly's recent behavior. "Why are you doing this? That kind of stuff makes it hard for me to be friends with you," Julia admitted.

Kimberly just rolled her eyes. "Who needs *you* anyway?" she snapped, stomping off.

Julia wondered what to do. She couldn't make Kimberly's choices for her. But Julia hated the idea of losing a friend who had been such a big part of her life.

Sadly, Julia decided not to hang out with Kimberly anymore. "Lord," Julia prayed softly, "please be with Kimberly and help her make choices that will give her a happy life. And please send me a new best friend."

More to Explore: "Do not set foot on the path of the wicked or walk in the way of evildoers. Avoid it, do not travel on it; turn from it and go on your way." (Proverbs 4:14 – 15)

Connecting to God: "Dear God, I'm lonely and would love to have a best friend. Please bring a new friend into my life, and help me to make a good choice. Amen."

Journal Prompt: What is the most important quality in a good friend?

Take Action: How can you identify a good and godly friend? Here are some traits:

> *Honesty* A true friend isn't a "yes" person. She will tell you encouraging things, but she will also kindly point out when you are making a mistake.

Loyalty A godly friend sticks by you, no matter what, and never is guilty of backstabbing.

Understanding A true friend doesn't mind listening to your problems or helping you find answers.

Sincerity A godly friend is not someone who only hangs around for what you can give them or do for them.

Positivity A good friend doesn't whine all the time, but instead is someone you can laugh with. She doesn't discourage you further, but instead encourages you during hard times.

Real-girl Confession: "My best friend is acting like a totally different person."

Indexed under: friendship, gossip, peer pressure

Devotion #14

"My heart pounds, my strength fails me; even the light has gone from my eyes. My friends and companions avoid me because of my wounds."

(Psalm 38:10 – 11)

Is Anyone There?

Lori felt like she'd rather die than go to school. Everyone knew what her dad had done last week. It was all over school. He was a coach and history teacher, and Lori hated running into him. Thank goodness she wasn't in any of his classes. She didn't know which was worse—the pain of being abandoned or the embarrassment that he'd left home and moved in with another woman.

Lori prayed all the time, begging God to help her family, but she secretly wondered if it did any good. Was God there? Why wasn't he bringing her dad back?

And what about her friends? Both Leah and Cheyenne avoided her now. Neither girl would even look her in the eye. Didn't they care about her pain? Mom said they were uncomfortable and embarrassed, and they didn't know what to say or how to help.

But that didn't make Lori feel any better. She needed her friends, even if she couldn't talk about the situation. She didn't want them to ignore her and pretend everything was okay.

One Sunday afternoon, Lori wandered from room to room, unable to decide what to do. If only she had someone to talk to! Mom was crying in her bedroom, and Dad was gone. Lori felt lonely and rejected and hopeless. She longed for someone to be with her, but no one was there.

She grabbed her jacket and headed out the door for a walk. The wind was brisk, and she hunched her shoulders as she headed into it. Mind deep in thought, Lori watched the leaves swirl around her feet and then blow on by.

After ten minutes, Lori glanced up in surprise. Her church building stood in front of her. She'd already walked three blocks!

Shivering in the wind, Lori decided to step inside. The door was still unlocked, and she slipped into the church and sat in a back pew. It felt strange being in the church alone. Strange, but peaceful too.

"Lori? Is that you?" a voice called from the shadows.

Lori whipped around. "Mrs. Layton?"

"Yes, it's me." Her Sunday school teacher sat beside her. "I was just putting up new bulletin boards in our classroom. What are you up to this afternoon?"

Lori hung her head. "I was just out walking, wishing I had ..." She stopped abruptly.

"Someone to talk to?" Mrs. Layton guessed.

"How did you know?" Lori asked, astonished.

"Oh, the church is the place people often come when they need a listening ear—either God's ear or a person's ear."

Lori only hesitated a moment before pouring out the pain in her heart. Mrs. Layton moved closer and put an arm around Lori's shoulders. "I'm so sorry this has happened to your family," she said. "Even if you're not sure it will help, keep talking to God. Tell him exactly how you feel. He will help you get through this tough period. In time, he will heal your loneliness."

Flipping through her Bible, Mrs. Layton found a verse to remind Lori that God would never leave her nor turn his back on her. Tears welled up in Lori's eyes. Even though she felt let down by her family and friends, Lori decided to trust that her heavenly Father *would* always be there for her. And when she needed someone, God would arrange for them to meet.

More to Explore: "I am exhausted from crying for help; my throat is parched. My eyes are swollen with weeping, waiting for my God to help me ... Answer my prayers, O LORD, for your unfailing love is wonderful. Take care of me, for your mercy is so plentiful." (Psalm 69:3,16 NLT)

Connecting to God: "Dear Lord, sometimes I wonder if you are really there or even hear my prayers. Things are really hard right now, and I feel like no one understands. Please, help me to keep praying and trusting you to answer. Amen."

Journal Prompt: What can you do to help keep yourself calm during tough times?

Take Action: Believe these true statements about what is happening:

This is a confusing, sad, and painful time for everyone.

The parent who left to live with another person has made his or her own choice.

You did not cause this — not in any way.

Real-girl Confession: "People look at me but then look away. I feel invisible."

Indexed under: abandonment, distant from God, friendship, loneliness, rejection

Devotion #15

Do you think I like people of the world who say "Yes" when they really mean "No?" As surely as God is faithful, our word to you does not waiver between "Yes" and "No."

(2 Corinthians 1:17–18 NLT)

Just Say What You Mean!

Hailey worked hard in study hall to finish her homework. She wanted it done because there was a movie on TV that night she'd been waiting to see. On the way home, she told her friend, Breanna, about it.

Breanna sighed. "I wish I could watch it too." She sighed again — even louder — and added, "But I have too much to do."

"Homework?" Hailey asked, afraid to hear the answer. She'd already helped Breanna with her reading and math homework twice that week. She wished Breanna worked more and goofed around less.

"Not just homework," Breanna said, dragging her feet. "I also have to weed Mom's flower garden for a party she's having *and* clean my room."

For some reason, Hailey felt guilty. "Do you want me to help you weed?"

"Oh, no," Breanna said, "you don't have to do that." She shifted her book bag to her other shoulder and sighed again. "I'll probably be up until midnight finishing my homework."

While I'm watching a movie, Hailey thought.

Hailey waved at the corner and walked the rest of the way home alone. One part of her felt guilty. If she was a good friend, shouldn't she help Breanna with all her work?

Another part of her was irritated. Breanna had written notes to friends all through study hall, while Hailey had worked. *I shouldn't have to bail her out again.*

Hailey stomped into the kitchen and dropped her book bag with a thud.

"Bad day?" Mom asked. "Want to tell me about it?" She listened as she folded a load of clothes.

Hailey repeated the conversation she'd had with Breanna. "What makes me the maddest, though, is that Breanna doesn't say what she means. She always says no when I offer to help, but she really means yes. What should I do?"

"Well, the Bible says our yes needs to mean yes, and our no needs to mean no," Mom explained. "We aren't supposed to say one thing when we mean another. That's not honest." She folded the last bath towel. "You can help Breanna be more honest by taking what she says at face value. If she says no, take it as if she really means no. If she wants something, wait until she asks directly with words. Ignore big sighs and sad looks. It just might help her be more honest."

Hailey decided to try once more. She called Breanna on the phone. "I could come over for an hour before supper and help weed the garden," she said. "Do you want me to?"

"No, you couldn't do much in just an hour," Breanna said, sounding dejected.

"Okay," Hailey said. "Hope you get everything done!" That night she enjoyed her movie—guilt-free.

More to Explore: "Just say a simple yes or no, so that you will not sin." (James 5:12 NLT)

Connecting to God: "Dear God, I don't understand why some people don't just say what they mean. Sometimes, I feel guilty about not doing what I know they really want me to do even though they won't say it. Help me to be honest and say what I mean — even when others don't. Amen."

Journal Prompt: Do you ever feel guilty even when you're certain you've done nothing wrong?

Take Action: Things to say and do when someone is pressuring you to do something you don't want to do:

> "I need to pray about this first." (This is *always* a good idea!)
>
> "I'll get back to you on that."
>
> "No, thanks, I don't want to."
>
> Use e-mail, voice mail, and texts to be straightforward.
>
> Don't get into arguments, defend your decision, or apologize. Stand in your truth!

Real-girl Confession: "I'm so tired of bailing her out!"

Indexed under: friendship, honesty

Devotion #16

"Do not be anxious about anything, but in every situation, by prayer and petition, with thanksgiving, present your requests to God."

(Philippians 4:6)

When the Future Is Scary

Hannah knew something was wrong the minute she walked through the door after school. Dad was home, sitting at the kitchen table with Mom. They stopped talking when Hannah entered the kitchen.

Hannah hugged them and asked, "Why are you home early, Dad? Are you sick?"

"No, I feel fine." He rubbed a hand over his face. "That's not exactly true. I don't feel fine." He paused. "I'm home early because I lost my job today."

"What?!" Hannah stared. "Why?"

"The company isn't doing well, and they had to cut some jobs," Dad said, "including mine."

"I'm sorry, Dad," Hannah said. "What's going to happen now? Will we have to move?" Hannah wondered whether they would even have food for next week. And what about her piano lessons? Hannah hated being selfish, but she'd once heard Mom tell Grandma how expensive the lessons were.

"I don't know what's going to happen now," Dad said, "but I do know one thing: Worrying doesn't help. It tangles up your brain so you can't think straight. God asks us to trust him instead. He'll take care of us." He smiled and put an arm around Hannah. "God will help me find another job."

"How?" Hannah asked.

"First, we'll give our worries to God," Mom said, pulling out another chair. "Why don't you join us?"

"Dear God," Dad prayed, "we thank you for whatever you have in mind during this time. You have promised to meet our needs, and we know you will. Show me where to look for work. I need a job. Help me to do my part, while I trust you to do your part. Amen."

Hannah studied her father's calm face. "Do you really feel okay?" she asked.

Dad nodded. "I trust God to take care of us. Worrying about what's going to happen just keeps us from doing our best *now*. We've prayed, and we're trusting God with the result. Now it's time to focus on doing what we need to do—today. God will take care of tomorrow."

Hannah smiled. If Dad could trust God with this problem, she could too.

More to Explore: "Give all your worries and cares to God, for he cares about you." (1 Peter 5:7 NLT)

Connecting to God: "Dear God, sometimes I worry about what's going to happen tomorrow. Help me to bring my worries to you and trust you to meet my needs. Thank you for taking care of them—and me! Amen."

Journal Prompt: What are your biggest money worries? Write a prayer letter, bringing those worries to God.

Take Action: When money is tight for your family, be sure to "shop smart."

Don't shop as a sport. When you hang out at the mall, you see things you don't need and buy them on a whim. But it's fun to simply admire stuff too — have some dressing-room fun or listen to new tracks in the music store.

Shop the sales. Get more for your money by hitting clearance racks and buy-one-get-one deals. But don't buy just because something is on sale. Do you really need it?

For gifts, shop in advance. Don't wait until the last minute when you're desperate. You might blow your budget because you've run out of time.

Shop outlets, discount stores, and thrift shops. Savvy shoppers can score cool vintage finds and real buys!

Real-girl Confession: "I'm embarrassed to admit that I can't afford it."

Indexed under: job loss, needs, worry

Devotion #17

"We can make our plans, but the LORD determines our steps."

(Proverbs 16:9 NLT)

Day of Disappointment

Zoe was counting the days until Catherine's birthday pool party. Zoe had bought a new swimsuit, and Catherine's gift was already wrapped. The party was being held at a country club swimming pool. Zoe couldn't wait to see it.

On the day of the party, Zoe and her dad left home in plenty of time. The country club was outside the city, and traffic was heavy on the interstate. Suddenly, a van cut into their lane and hit them. Their car crashed through the guardrail and landed in a ditch.

Zoe and her dad weren't hurt, but they had to sit by the road for an hour while police officers took statements and called a tow truck. *"Dad!"* Zoe complained. "The party will be over before I get there! Can't you make them hurry?"

"I'm sorry, Zoe," Dad said, "but there's nothing I can do. I have to stay here until the truck comes, and since Mom's out of town, she can't come get you."

"But it's not fair!" Zoe cried.

"I know how frustrating it is to have something ruined by circumstances you have no control over." He put an arm around her and pulled her close. "But the main thing to think about right now is being grateful to God that no one was badly hurt."

"I know … but I was really looking forward to this party."

Dad nodded. "It's disappointing when something wrecks your plans. But don't let it ruin the rest of your weekend."

Zoe chewed her lower lip. That was easy for him to say. He hadn't been invited to the best party of the summer.

"It might be hard to believe right now," Dad said, "but God has a plan he's working out, even now. Proverbs says a man makes many plans, but God may direct your steps another way. God's purpose in this will stand firm."

"What purpose?" Zoe asked.

"I don't know yet," Dad admitted. "Maybe we'll never know. But you can trust that God has your best interests at heart—even now."

An hour later, the tow truck finally came—and Zoe went home with Dad in a cab.

Zoe missed the birthday party, but when she heard about it the next day, she no longer minded. Some kids had started a big fight, smashing some furniture, and the party had broken up early. Zoe was very sorry for Catherine, but she was glad she'd missed the party.

More to Explore: "The very steps we take come from GOD; otherwise how would we know where we're going?" (Proverbs 20:24 MSG)

Connecting to God: "Dear God, I get really disappointed and upset when something ruins my plans. When that happens, help me to stop, take a deep breath, pray, and trust you even though I don't understand the reason why. Amen."

Journal Prompt: Is there another way I can look at what happened?

Take Action: What to do when God interrupts your plans:

Ask. Ask God for his point of view about what happened.

Listen. Hear God's answer through reading your Bible and listening in your spirit.

Surrender. Ask for God's will to be done instead of asking him to meet your desires.

Wait. Be patient and see how God's plan works out.

Real-girl Confession: "I have to do something to change this — now!"

Indexed under: disappointment

Devotion #18

"Do not let your heart be troubled, nor let it be fearful."

(John 14:27 NASB)

A Troubled Heart

Joy rolled over in bed, shut off her alarm, and groaned. She'd had more than the usual number of nightmares of cars crashing. She pressed a fist into her sore stomach. Was she too young to have an ulcer? Joy muffled a groan and sat up.

How ironic that her name was *Joy*. She couldn't remember the last time she'd felt any.

At breakfast, Joy gritted her teeth. How could Sammie, her little sister, be so chirpy and cheerful? *Can't you just shut up?* Joy thought. At least Sammie got Mom's attention long enough for Joy to slide her bagel and eggs into the trash compactor. She just couldn't swallow anything this morning.

On the way to school, Sammie jumped around in her booster seat. "You're shaking the whole back seat!" Joy snapped. "Stop it!"

"Are you okay?" Mom asked, peering at Joy in the rearview mirror.

"Yes, but—Mom, look out!" Joy screeched.

Mom swerved to miss a squirrel in the street, then swerved back before hitting a parked car. "Joy! For heaven's sake! You almost caused an accident! Don't scream in my ear."

"Sorry," Joy mumbled, her stomach rolling like she might throw up. She swallowed hard as fear washed over her in waves. She'd almost caused her mom to be in a car crash ... just like she'd caused Dad's wreck.

Even Sammie was quiet the rest of the way to school. Before getting out of the car, Joy reached over the front seat and patted her mom's shoulder. "You'll be careful, won't you?" she asked.

Mom turned around, a puzzled look on her face. "Of course, I will. You don't need to worry about me. Remember what Jesus said? 'Don't let your heart be troubled or afraid.' I'll be praying for you today."

"Okay, thanks." Joy hopped out of the car and slammed the door.

"Good luck on your test today. I know you'll do great—you're a whiz at math."

I used to be, Joy thought, but not lately. Mom would find out soon enough that her math grade—all her grades—had slipped. She couldn't concentrate anymore, not even on her favorite puzzles or games or books. She could barely stay awake some days.

Nothing was the same since Dad died in that fiery car crash a year ago. He'd been on the way to pick up Joy's bike at the repair shop when a drunk driver hit him. Even though Mom didn't blame her, Joy knew the accident was her fault. Dad was there because of *her* bike.

That day after school, Mrs. Gonzales called Joy to her desk. "I need to talk to you about the math test today," she said. "Before this goes on any longer, I'd like to get you some help."

"A math tutor?" Joy asked, embarrassed that her teacher thought she was that far behind.

"No, I was thinking of a counselor to help you work through your grief," Mrs. Gonzales said. "The school counselor, or maybe someone your mother would choose."

Joy hunched her shoulders. "Mom wanted me to see the counselor who works at our church," she admitted. Joy stared at the D- on her test. "Things have been hard since Dad died." She gulped. "But I think I'm ready to talk about it."

It took several months of talking and praying—and crying—before Joy could tell a difference. Gradually, the nightmares stopped, her appetite picked up, and she was able to concentrate again. She even enjoyed playing with her little sister. Joy was grateful to God to have her joy back.

More to Explore: "The LORD will give strength to His people; the LORD will bless His people with peace." (Psalm 29:11 NKJV)

Connecting to God: "Dear God, I can't stop being sad and angry and afraid about what happened. Please give me strength to go on every day. Help me find someone to talk to about this. Amen."

Journal Prompt: Write a letter to a person who died and list the things you miss most about that person.

Take Action: If you have a friend who is grieving the loss of someone...

Practice saying or writing a comforting message: "Leila, I am so sorry about your father. I know you will miss him very much. Let me know if I can help you with your homework project or anything else."

Remain friends. Even normal social activities such as inviting a friend over to play, going to the park, riding bikes, or watching a movie can offer a much-needed distraction.

Real-girl Confession: "I'm never going to feel any better."

Indexed under: death, fear, worry

Devotion #19

"Anger is cruel, and wrath is like a flood, but jealousy is even more dangerous."

(Proverbs 27:4 NLT)

Secret Jealousy

Jasmine felt guilty because she couldn't stand her little sister. It wasn't Emma's fault, but Jasmine was jealous of her. Emma had been in and out of hospitals her whole life. Jasmine knew she should feel sorry for Emma, but Jasmine boiled with anger over all the attention Emma got.

Church members brought her stuffed animals and candy. Neighbors loaned her DVDs to watch. Mom and Dad held Emma constantly. Even when they weren't actually with her, they talked about Emma's condition all the time.

Hey, you have another girl! Jasmine wanted to yell. *Remember me?*

One day after school, her teacher stopped her in the hall-way. "I've been meaning to ask you. How's your little sister doing these days?"

Jasmine slammed her locker door hard, and then looked horrified. "Sorry, Mrs. Johnson."

"Is something wrong?" she asked.

Jasmine shook her head no, but tears welled up in her eyes. She brushed them away in embarrassment.

Mrs. Johnson guided her back into the empty classroom. "Has your sister's health gotten worse? Is that the trouble?" she asked kindly.

"No," Jasmine whispered. She had no intention of telling her teacher what was wrong. But when Jasmine looked up at her teacher's sympathetic expression, the words started pouring from her. Soon she had dumped out all her hurt feelings and hateful thoughts.

Mrs. Johnson got her a tissue and waited while Jasmine wiped her eyes. "What you're feeling about your sister is totally normal," she said. "Brothers and sisters often feel jealous of the attention a sibling receives."

"How I feel is *normal*?" Jasmine asked in disbelief.

"Yes, but even though it's perfectly natural, you must deal with the jealousy. If you don't, it will eat away inside you." She patted Jasmine's hand. "Your bitterness will damage your relationship with your sister—and maybe with your parents, too."

Mrs. Johnson outlined the steps Jasmine could take, if she wanted, to get rid of the jealousy. Jasmine slowly nodded. "Okay. I'll try your plan."

"It's not *my* plan actually," Mrs. Johnson said, smiling. "It's from the Bible. It's God's plan, and you can trust it."

Right then, Jasmine asked God to forgive her for her anger and jealousy about Emma. Jasmine asked God to fill her with his love for Emma so that she could show real love to her little sister.

The last step of the plan was the hardest. That night, Jasmine went to her parents. Through her tears, she told them how she felt. "I don't want to feel jealous of Emma, but I get lonely when you seem to forget about me. I know I don't have really big problems like Emma does, but I still need your attention sometimes."

Jasmine's parents were very glad she had spoken up. They began spending more time with Jasmine — and Jasmine grew to treasure her younger sister.

More to Explore: "For wherever there is jealousy and selfish ambition, there you will find disorder and evil of every kind." (James 3:16 NLT)

Connecting to God: "Dear God, I know my family loves me, but sometimes it's hard to remember that I'm important to them. Please take away my jealous feelings. Amen."

Journal Prompt: Physical activities can help emotions be more positive. What physical activities help you control your feelings?

Take Action: Jealousy has been called "the green-eyed monster." Here's how to conquer that monster!

1. Confess the sin of jealousy to God. He will understand — and forgive.

2. Ask God to fill you with love for the other person.

3. Talk to the people involved. Getting the problem out in the open is an important step in healing it.

Real-girl Confession: "It hurts that my dad loves my brother more than me."

Indexed under: anger, honesty, jealousy

Devotion #20

"I will say of the LORD, 'He is my refuge and my fortress, my God, in whom I trust."

(Psalm 91:2)

"I'm Afraid"

"Mom?" Amanda said. "You have to do something about Conner."

Mom frowned and stopped slicing carrots. "What's wrong?"

Amanda popped a carrot slice into her mouth. "He won't tell you, but he's scared all the time, and he's driving me crazy with his weird behavior."

Mom laid down her knife. "What weird behavior?"

Amanda chose her words carefully. "Conner's been having nightmares since Dad started his new trucking job and is gone all week. He's too embarrassed to tell you. He thinks being eight is so grown-up." Amanda shrugged. "But he wakes me up nearly every night, sneaking into my room to sleep on the floor."

"I didn't know that! Did he say what he's afraid of?"

"He's scared someone will break in during the night. He's afraid after school too, until you get home from work. He follows me around the house and practically sits on me when I'm doing homework."

Mom wrapped an arm around Amanda. "Thank you so much for telling me, hon."

That night after supper, Mom took both Conner and Amanda around the house, showing them the locks on the doors and windows. When Conner said he was most nervous about their sliding glass door, Mom blocked it with a steel bar in the track at the bottom. Then it couldn't be opened. She also gave Conner and Amanda the phone numbers of several neighbors.

"There's another list of numbers taped to the refrigerator by the phone," Mom added.

Last of all, they each pretended to call 9-1-1 in case of emergency. They practiced stating the problem and their address very slowly and clearly.

Before bed, Mom prayed with Conner and Amanda. "Remember that God is watching over us day and night. We can totally trust him."

"Does that mean that nothing bad will ever happen to us now?" Conner asked.

Mom smiled. "That would be nice, but no. Although, we are always under divine protection. God will either intervene and stop bad things from happening to us, or he will help us be strong as we go through them. Either way, he is always with us to help."

More to Explore: "You will keep in perfect peace all who trust in you, all whose thoughts are fixed on you! Trust in the LORD always, for the LORD GOD is the eternal Rock."(Isaiah 26: 3 – 4 NLT)

Connecting to God: "Dear Lord, sometimes I'm afraid when I have to be alone. I worry about what might happen. Instead, help me remember that you are my protector and will show me what to do. I trust you to take care of me. Help me to keep my thoughts on you. Amen."

Journal Prompt: Can you remember a time when you were afraid and God helped you?

Take Action: If you're afraid when home alone, try these tips:

Turn on the TV or listen to music.

As parents leave, lock and check all windows and doors.

Have a friend come over to hang out.

Keep a phone within reach.

Turn on all lights at night, inside and out.

With permission, let your dog or cat come inside.

Real-girl Confession: "When I'm home alone, the littlest sound freaks me out!"

Indexed under: change, fear, honesty

Devotion #21

"You put the down-and-out on their feet and protect the unprotected from bullies!"

(Psalm 35:10 MSG)

"Help!"

On Danielle's school bus, an older boy had targeted her to pick on. He kept taking her backpack away from her. Once he "accidentally" hit Danielle so hard that she banged her head against the window. Twice, he stole her lunch money.

"Can't you drive me to school?" Danielle begged her mom.

"I can't," Mom said. "My job starts at the same time as school, but on the opposite side of town." She paused. "Is something wrong?"

"This older boy picks on me a lot." Tears filled Danielle's eyes. "I tell the driver sometimes, but the boy keeps doing it when no one is looking. Mostly, he takes my stuff."

"Hmm ..." Mom tilted her head. "How many more times do you want to put up with this? Once more? Twice? Ten times?"

Danielle's eyes opened wide. "I *don't* put up with it! I try to get away from him!"

"I imagine that this bully enjoys seeing you afraid or crying. It makes him feel powerful." Mom looked Danielle in the eye. "You must stop giving away your confidence."

"What? How?"

"God promises to protect you against bullies." Mom opened her Bible. "And Isaiah 30:15 tells you how to act: 'In quietness and confidence shall be your strength.'"

"I don't get it," Danielle said.

"You tell this bully in a calm, confident voice that you won't stand for his behavior anymore. Tell him if it happens *at all* again, your mom will talk to his parents and the principal, and if necessary, the police. Look him right in the eye, say it with confidence, then sit down and say no more. That's quiet confidence."

"I don't know . . ."

"We'll practice together until you can do it."

"What if he takes my money anyway?"

"Then, we follow through immediately on what you promised. I'll talk to the necessary authorities." Mom gave her a hug. "And, Danielle, thank you for telling me about this. I know it's hard, but we can deal with this together. Your safety is so important to me."

The next morning, the boy took Danielle's flute. Danielle's knees trembled, but her voice was strong when she delivered the speech she'd practiced. The bully glared at her and called her a name, but gave the flute back. To Danielle's amazement, he left her alone after that.

More to Explore: "He delivered me from my strong enemy, from those who hated me, for they were too strong for me." (Psalm 18:17 NKJV)

Connecting to God: "Dear God, there are some scary people in my life. Help me to be calm and stand up to bullies. Thank you for protecting me. Help me remember that you're always with me, watching over me. Amen."

Journal Prompt: Journaling about feelings and behavior can help you see patterns that happen over and over. Why is noticing patterns helpful?

Take Action: Everyday tips for dealing with bullies:

Do not respond by fighting or bullying back. It can grow quickly into violence.

Avoid the bully whenever possible.

Use the buddy system. Be with a friend on the bus, in the hallways, or at recess — wherever the bully is.

Use a different bathroom if a bully is nearby.

Don't go to your locker when there is nobody around.

Try not to react by crying or looking upset.

Practice reacting with a calm demeanor.

Control your anger. Practice "cool down" strategies such as counting to ten, taking deep breaths, or walking away.

Keep a straight face. Smiling or laughing may provoke the bully.

Firmly and clearly tell the bully to stop, then walk away and ignore the bully.

Tell an adult. Teachers, principals, parents, bus drivers, or lunchroom monitors can help.

Remove reasons for the bullying. If the bully is demanding your lunch money, start bringing your lunch. If he's trying to get your music player, don't bring it to school.

Real-girl Confession: "He turned riding the bus into my worst nightmare."

Indexed under: bullies, fear, honesty, secrets

Devotion #22

"There is a path before each person that seems right, but it ends in death."

(Proverbs 14:12 NLT)

Dumped!

Elizabeth was best friends with Abigail—that is, until Natalie moved in next door to Abigail. Suddenly, it was Abigail and Natalie walking to and from school together. When Elizabeth called Abigail on Saturdays, she already had fun plans with Natalie.

Elizabeth told her mom about the situation. "Don't worry," Mom said. "Friendships change. Abigail isn't doing anything wrong by making more friends. Maybe you'll like Natalie when you get to know her better."

But one day, Natalie stopped Elizabeth at school and said, "Why don't you leave Abigail alone? She's my best friend now. She's too nice to tell you, but she wants you to stop calling her."

Elizabeth blinked back tears, determined not to cry in front of the new girl. But Natalie's words hurt deeply. How could Abigail dump her like that? The more Elizabeth thought about it, the worse she felt. Then she got mad. Really mad. She'd show Abigail how it felt to be left out!

For many months, Elizabeth and Abigail had been planning a camping trip for Elizabeth's birthday in June. Elizabeth's family had even rented a cabin in the mountains.

"Abigail's not coming now," Elizabeth said to her parents. Abigail needed to know how it felt to be left out. Elizabeth would do it back to her. She enjoyed writing a note to tell Abigail that she was no longer invited on the mountain vacation. Elizabeth would ask someone else instead.

Come June, Elizabeth didn't enjoy having someone else on her birthday trip—the other girl complained about everything. Then Elizabeth found out Natalie had lied to her. Abigail had actually wanted to be friends with *both* girls.

"God, what should I do now?" Elizabeth prayed. "I miss my best friend."

For direction, Elizabeth turned to God's Word, which says she should forgive her enemies and even pray for them. That meant Natalie too. The Bible also says not to pay people back for the wrong things they've done. Even though it was hard to do, Elizabeth decided to do it God's way. As she prayed to forgive Natalie, peace slowly filled her heart. It was like quenching a raging fire.

Elizabeth knew she wasn't finished yet. She also wrote a note to Abigail, asking forgiveness for taking back the vacation invitation.

Eventually, all three girls became friends. Elizabeth was glad she'd ultimately handled the situation God's way.

More to Explore: "Fools think their own way is right, but the wise listen to others." (Proverbs 12:15 NLT)

Connecting to God: "Dear God, help me adjust when my friendships go through changes. Forgive me for the times I've been mean to others, and help me to forgive others who have hurt me. Amen."

Journal Prompt: Write about this anonymous saying: "You don't have to change friends if you understand that friends change."

Take Action: Remember that friendships can and do change ...

Friendship means understanding, not agreement.

Friendship means forgiveness, not resentment.

Friendship means the memories last, even if contact is lost.

Just because a friendship didn't last forever, doesn't mean it wasn't worthwhile.

Real-girl Confession: "Where did my BFF go?"

Indexed under: abandonment, friendship, revenge

Devotion #23

"One thing I do: Forgetting what is behind and straining toward what is ahead, I press on . . ."

(Philippians 3:13 – 14)

Weekends Will Never Be the Same

Emmy used to love Saturdays. When her dad was still alive, they worked in their backyard garden together. They biked on a nearby trail. They played baseball—he'd been teaching Emmy how to pitch. But one day when biking, Dad was hit by a driver who never saw him. Now he was gone.

Emmy and her mom had to move into a tiny upstairs apartment with a dinky balcony and no garden. Emmy hated Saturdays now. When she woke up on Saturday, she was excited . . . until she remembered Dad was gone. Then she was miserable.

"I know you're sad, Emmy. I'm very sad too," Mom said. "But we need to stop thinking so much about how things used to be. The Bible calls it 'forgetting what lies behind us.'"

"But I don't want to forget Dad!"

"Of course not. We will *never* forget him, but it doesn't help to focus on our old routines that are gone now." She hugged Emmy close. "We both need to pay more attention to the future, 'straining toward what lies ahead' instead."

"I don't know how to do that. Do you?" Emmy asked.

"Well, let's start with today. Our Saturdays are very different now, but they can still be good. How can we make them fun? Let's make a list of the ways."

Over the next month, Emmy and her mom tried some different things. In a few months, they had a new Saturday routine. They went out for a donut for breakfast, took a trip to the library, and finished the morning doing a Bible study together in a park. After some chores at home, they went to an afternoon movie at the dollar theater. It wasn't easy at first because Emma still felt sad on Saturdays. But over time, their new routine became fun, and Emmy began to love weekends again.

One Saturday morning while munching a donut, Emmy remarked, "Things are getting a little better, aren't they?"

Mom nodded. "Change isn't easy. It hasn't happened overnight for us." She licked some chocolate frosting from her fingers. "We just have to keep going."

"Even when it feels hard," Emmy added.

"Especially then. The Bible says life can be like a race. If you do your very best and don't give up, you'll win the prize." She grabbed her purse and stood. "I think our prize was discovering that focusing on a bright future can bring us some *good* things."

More to Explore: "Do you not know that in a race all the runners run, but only one gets the prize? Run in such a way as to get the prize." (1 Corinthians 9:24 NIV)

Connecting to God: "Dear God, thank you for being with me during sad times of change. I need help to stop looking back. Help me to be patient and grateful for the good things you're bringing into my life. Amen."

Journal Prompt: Thinking about a loss too much can deepen your sadness into depression. What true positive thoughts can you focus on to lift your spirits?

Take Action: Helpful ways to deal with grief:

Talk openly and honestly with a trusted adult about your loss.

Cry when you need to — expressing grief helps you heal.

Express your grief in ways you find meaningful: journaling, writing poetry, art, or music.

Create a memorial for your loved one, perhaps by planting a special tree or bush.

Real-girl Confession: "It feels like the sadness will go on forever."

Indexed under: change, death, sadness

Devotion #24

"I have heard the many rumors about me ... My enemies conspire against me ... But I am trusting you, O LORD!"

(Psalm 31:13 – 14 NLT)

Stabbed in the Back

Karyn was excited that she'd made the junior cheerleading squad at her new school. Karyn looked forward to becoming friends with the other three cheerleaders. That is, until the girl who shared her locker gave her a warning.

"Talk about gossip girls!" She rolled her eyes. "Those cheerleaders are backbiters. They'll eat you alive."

Karyn's stomach clenched, but she forced a smile, pretending her locker mate was just kidding. If Karyn didn't talk nasty about the other girls, surely they wouldn't treat her that way.

The next day at practice, the other cheerleaders made nasty comments about one girl's weight, another girl's hair, and a boy's shabby clothes. Karyn held back. Their talk made her uncomfortable.

Still, she wanted to be friends with these girls. They were popular and pretty. If they liked Karyn, then they'd make sure she was included in things.

So Karyn decided to just remain quiet. She wouldn't join in the gossip. She'd just listen.

Karyn walked home with them after school, but after two blocks, she regretted it. They didn't have anything nice to say about *anyone* in school—kids or teachers. Karyn dragged her feet and fell behind.

"You're awfully quiet," Brittany said, waiting for Karyn. "Are you shocked by the number of uncool creeps in this school?"

"Uh, no," Karyn said.

The others turned to stare at her. "No?" Brittany said. "What do you mean, *no*?"

"Well, I *like* most of my teachers," Karyn said quietly. "And I like the girl who shares my locker."

Brittany and her friends snickered. Then Brittany said, "You know something, Karyn? I don't think you're going to fit in with us after all."

Karyn studied the girls. A verse from youth group popped into her mind, and she grinned. "You know something, Brittany? I don't think so either." She turned the corner and headed toward home, whispering the verse. "No good is going to come from that crowd ..."

Tomorrow she'd eat lunch with her locker mate—and get to know her better.

More to Explore: "I have heard the many rumors about me." (Jeremiah 20:10 NLT)

Connecting to God: "Dear God, sometimes it's tempting to join in with gossip just to feel like I belong. But I know it's wrong and only hurts others. Help me to turn away from it instead. Amen."

Journal Prompt: What do you think about this quote? "Gossip, as usual, was one-third right and two-thirds wrong." L.M. Montgomery, *Chronicles of Avonlea (Anne of Green Gables* series)

Take Action: *Steps to Stopping Gossip*

1. Don't take part in any gossiping whatsoever.
2. If someone tries to engage you in gossip, calmly change the subject.
3. Deny a rumor if anyone asks, but don't go out of your way to discuss it.
4. Live your life so people will know any rumor isn't true.
5. Forgive the gossipers and forget about revenge.
6. Go about your day with confidence.
7. If gossiping continues or worsens, report it to a teacher or principal.

Real-girl Confession: "They're totally insensitive and mean. I don't think they even care about the people they talk about."

Indexed under: friendship, gossip

Devotion #25

"People ruin their lives by their own foolishness and then are angry at the LORD."

(Proverbs 19:3 NLT)

Paying Consequences

Michelle suited up in the locker room, admiring her new basketball shoes. She couldn't wait to start practice. She'd grown two inches since last winter and was no longer the shortest person on the team.

She'd also practiced all summer, shooting free throws and dribbling with both hands. She couldn't wait to show the coach how she'd improved. Thanks to her, they'd have a much better chance for a winning season.

Coach Morales divided them into two teams. "Everybody on the floor! Let's see what you remember from last year."

Up and down the gym floor they ran. Michelle had even more fun than she'd expected. She dribbled around and through the opposing side, changing hands easily. She shot baskets from the free throw line twice and *swish!* In they went!

When the coach blew the whistle, Michelle's team was ahead 12–2. She smiled to herself. She'd made ten of those points herself!

Lined up on the bench, Michelle listened as Coach Morales praised them for all the things they'd done right. "We're looking good for a first practice," he said. "There's just one thing I want to remind you of."

He waited until all eyes were focused on him.

"What does the word 'team' mean?" he asked.

"A group?" Maya said.

"A squad?" Nina asked.

"Both are right," Coach said. "But a team is a group or squad who works together. Each person is important. No one is the star." He looked at Michelle. "You've obviously worked hard on your basketball skills, Michelle. Just remember, though, to pass the ball around. The game isn't about *you*. It's about the team working together."

Michelle's face grew hot. What a rotten thing to say to her! "I just want us to win," she said. "Why should I pass the ball to someone who will miss the shot when I know I can make it?"

Coach Morales frowned. "First of all, you have no idea how much the other girls have also practiced their skills. And second, I'd rather have a team who works well together than one that wins because of a hotshot player who hogs the ball."

"That's stupid!" Michelle jumped up. "I'm not playing on some losing team after all the work I did!" She stomped off to the locker room. Fuming, she heard the girls running as practice continued. She had changed clothes by the time the other girls came in.

She had also calmed down and regretted her outburst. She really wanted to play on the team. Michelle took a deep breath. She'd need to apologize.

Michelle walked out to the gym and waited. Coach Morales glanced at her, but said nothing and continued to write on his clipboard. Heart pounding, Michelle walked across the gym floor and cleared her throat. "I'm sorry about what I said," Michelle said. "I *do* want to play on the team."

"I'm sorry you chose to be rude like that too," Coach said, clutching his clipboard. "I can't have that kind of behavior on the team though. Sorry."

Michelle gulped. "You mean I can't play?"

"Not right away, no. You'll sit on the bench the first three games."

Michelle stomped her foot. "That's not fair!"

Coach shook his head. "There are consequences for behavior, Michelle. There's no point in getting angry at me. You brought this on yourself. You've worked on your basketball skills. Now see what you can do about managing your anger."

More to Explore: "For the LORD sees clearly what a man does, examining every path he takes." (Proverbs 5:21 NLT)

Connecting to God: "Dear God, I'm sorry for how I acted. I wish I didn't have to pay the price for my actions. Let me remember what my anger might cost me — and help me control it. Amen."

Journal Prompt: If you saw someone your age having a temper tantrum, what would you think? What do you suppose others are thinking when *you* blow up?

Take Action: Godly ways Michelle could have handled things differently:

"I'm sorry I was rude, Coach. Is there anything I can do to make up for this?"

"Even if I can't practice with the team, can I come and watch? Then I can practice my skills at home and keep up."

[in the locker room with the team] "I'm sorry I hogged the ball today, and I'm sorry I made it sound like I'm better than the rest of you."

Real-girl Confession: "I felt like dying when those words flew out of my mouth!"

Indexed under: anger, rebellion

Devotion #26

"Come aside by yourselves to a deserted place and rest a while."

(Mark 6:31 NKJV)

Come Apart Before You Come Apart

Josie's mom had cancer. She was going to get better, the doctors said, but it had been a tough year. Mom had been very sick, then had surgery, and then drove to the hospital every week for treatments that made her even sicker for a while. During the year, Josie had gone to school, kept up with homework, done most of the housework, including laundry and dishes, and entertained her little brother. Most nights, she dropped into bed too tired to worry—and often fell asleep during her prayers.

Even though Josie was glad to help, one day she felt almost too tired to crawl out of bed. The thought of getting herself—and her brother—ready for school seemed overwhelming. And after school she had a Girl Scout meeting and then there would be homework ... and then supper to cook ... and on it went. Josie sighed. She wanted to crawl back under the covers. She just couldn't face the day ahead.

That afternoon, the mother of Josie's best friend gave her a ride home from the Girl Scout meeting. "My, you look exhausted," Mrs. Whitely said when Josie climbed into the car. "I know it's tough at home right now."

Josie nodded. "Some days, I can't even remember what day it is."

"I can imagine." Mrs. Whitely drove in silence for a block. "You know, God understands how you feel," she said. "He knows you need rest. You should take breaks — often."

Josie sighed. "I wish I could, but how?"

"For the time being, choose more restful activities." She pulled into Josie's driveway. "Next week, you could skip the Girl Scout meeting and do something more restful instead. What do you find relaxing?"

"Reading a good book," Josie said immediately, "but there hasn't been time for that lately."

"Tomorrow at school, go to the library and find a good book," Mrs. Whitley said. "At home, take fifteen minutes every day and read, or go for a walk alone — or stay home and take a nap." She gave Josie a big hug. "I know you're responsible for a lot. It's okay to get away from it all for a while. God is still in control, and he will take care of things while you rest!"

More to Explore: "Come to me, all you who are weary and burdened, and I will give you rest." (Matthew 11:28)

Connecting to God: "Dear God, I feel overwhelmed, and I'm so tired I could drop. Please show me how I can rest now, and thank you for renewing my strength. Amen."

Journal Prompt: Being upset uses a lot of energy — and you might not have much to spare. How can you stop this "energy leak"?

Take Action: Dealing with Fatigue:

Get enough sleep Get at least eight hours (nine is better) of sleep each night.

Exercise Try walking, biking, or swimming.

Eat smart Consume more protein, fruits, and vegetables — and less sugar and caffeine.

Journal When stress feels overwhelming, write down your feelings.

Pray Talk to God about what's happening and what you need. Pray often!

Real-girl Confession: "I'm so tired I feel as old as my grandma."

Indexed under: needs, overloaded

Devotion #27

"You, O LORD, are a shield around me."

(Psalm 3:3 NLT)

Beware! Online Danger

Angie pulled out her homework folder and headed to the computer. If she got her science report finished before Mom got home from work, she could go skating with Corinda before dark.

She Googled her topic of cell division, read the list of website choices, and opened three sites using separate tabs. Angie glanced at the clock. She could spend half an hour reading the articles and taking notes. Ten minutes to outline her article and twenty minutes to write a rough draft would get her finished right on time.

Halfway through reading the first article, a pop-up window appeared. It offered a free science report if she gave her name and e-mail address. *The article sounds really helpful*, Angie thought. She filled in the information, clicked "OK," and went back to reading her article.

When she checked her e-mail's inbox for her free science report, Angie was shocked and scared. Instead of a science report, someone had used her e-mail address to send her some awful pictures and called her a very mean name. Shaking with fear, Angie clicked "delete" and closed her e-mail.

Angie wrapped her arms around herself, but she kept shivering. The words on the computer screen blurred. Then she raised her gaze to a framed picture above the computer, put there by her mom. The Bible verse said, "The Lord is my strength, my shield from every danger."

Even though the nasty e-mail couldn't physically hurt her, Angie felt in danger just the same. "Lord, please help me know what to do," she whispered. "Be my shield and protect me from this danger."

By the time Mom came home from work, Angie had decided what to do. "Mom, I forgot the rule about not filling in personal information on the computer," she said.

Mom sat down beside her. "Tell me about it."

Angie told her story.

"Show me the e-mail," Mom said.

"I can't. I was so upset that I deleted it."

"I'll find it," Mom said. She got into Angie's e-mail, went to the trash folder, and found it. "This is mean and disgusting, and I'm so sorry this happened to you. I'm going to report this incident to our Internet provider."

"I'm sorry I forgot the rule," Angie said. "I'll remember next time."

More to Explore: "The LORD is my strength and shield. I trust him with all my heart." (Psalm 28:7 NLT)

Connecting to God: "Lord, I love being online, but sometimes I see or hear things that scare me. Please shield me from things that could hurt me, and help me remember and obey the safety rules. Amen."

Journal Prompt: Do you follow your family's online safety rules, even when your parents are not around? If not, why not?

Take Action: You've met someone in a science chat room approved by your parents and teacher. You two share cooking experiments and recipes. One day, the girl (who claims she is your age) asks if you can get together. She suggests meeting in a small park in your town. What is a good response to this invitation?

1. Ask your parent or guardian for permission.
2. Change the meeting place to one with many people around, like a mall.
3. Take your parent or guardian along to the meeting.
4. All of the above.

Real-girl Confession: "I love being online with my friends."

Indexed under: abuse/emotional/verbal, fear

Devotion #28

"Human anger does not produce the righteousness that God desires."

(James 1:20)

Not Again!

Isabel hurried through the kitchen on the way to her room to pack for the weekend. She almost bumped into Mom, who was on the phone and looking irritated.

"Yes, I understand that these things happen," Mom finally said, her voice sounding surprisingly calm. "Part of a weekend is better than no weekend." She paused and took a deep breath. "Yes, I'll tell her. I'll enjoy having Isabel home tonight." She hung up.

Isabel's nostrils flared. "Dad's not coming *again?*" She threw her backpack across the floor. "What is it this time?"

"He has a flat tire and no spare. By the time he finds someone to repair his flat, it will be too late to come tonight. He'll be here in the morning."

"I don't believe him!" Isabel screamed. "He found something more fun to do tonight! I hate him!"

"Whoa! Hold on a minute. Take a deep breath." Mom shook her head. "Letting your anger explode won't help you do the right thing."

"What's the right thing?" Isabel demanded.

95

"I think you know." Mom raised one eyebrow. "Be patient. Give him the benefit of the doubt. It's okay to be mad when you're disappointed—at me or Dad," Mom said slowly. "And it's okay to say so." She pulled Isabel close. "But it's *not* okay to say hurtful things."

"If he did stuff like that to you, you'd say bad things too!" Isabel said.

"Well, to tell the truth, I'm irritated about it too," Mom said. "I'm supposed to go to a movie with my friend Janice tonight, and now I need to disappoint her. But screaming hurtful things at your dad would only have made it worse."

"That's true." Isabel nodded slowly. "I'm sorry you're missing the movie tonight."

"That's all right. I love that you're here." Mom paused. "Would you mind if we invite Janice over to watch a DVD with us? She's alone tonight."

Isabel grinned. "If we can make caramel popcorn too!"

More to Explore: "A hot-tempered person stirs up conflict, but the one who is patient calms a quarrel." (Proverbs 15:18)

Connecting to God: "Dear God, sometimes I get so mad I could scream. Help me find a godly way to handle my anger so I don't hurt others—or myself. Amen."

Journal Prompt: How do you respond when angry? Do you withdraw and clam up? Explode with angry words? Do you pretend you're fine but find sneaky ways to pay someone back?

Take Action: It's perfectly normal to be angry. It's okay to say, "I feel *really* mad." But before you act out your anger, follow these steps!

1. Get a change of scenery. Go outside, walk to a friend's house, or go to your room. Hanging around and throwing a fit only makes it worse.

2. Do something that calms you. Listen to music, go for a run, or even tackle that messy closet.

3. Have some fun. Read a good book. Watch a funny show. Call a friend and laugh.

4. After you're calm, tell the person why you were upset, but do it without blame or sarcasm.

Real-girl Confession: "I couldn't believe Dad would blow me off like that!"

Indexed under: anger, divorce

Devotion #29

"Finally, I confessed all my sins to you and stopped trying to hide my guilt. I said to myself, 'I will confess my rebellion to the LORD.' And you forgave me! All my guilt is gone."

(Psalm 32:5 NLT)

The Meltdown Solution

Sara's parents had agreed to "sharing" her equally after the divorce. She spent one week at Mom's, and then one week at Dad's. When she stayed at Mom's house, Sara walked to school with her best friend across the street. When at Dad's apartment, she had to take two different buses to school. She hated going back and forth. She was tired of leaving clothes or books at one home when she needed them at her other home.

One morning when she got to school, Sara realized her book bag was still on the bus. It held her gym clothes and a book report that was due. She called Dad at work, but he was in a meeting. By the time he got her message, found her book bag, and brought it to school, it was lunchtime.

"What took you so long?" Sara demanded. "I needed that stuff first period!"

"Take it easy," Dad said. "I'm not the one who left your book bag on the bus. Maybe you should thank me for bringing it to school."

Sara's heart pounded so hard her chest hurt. "*Thank* you? For what? The divorce wasn't my fault—it was yours! It's your fault I have to ride that stupid bus! I hate going to your dinky apartment!" She grabbed her book bag, turned around, and ran to class.

Sara was calmer an hour later, and the heaviness of guilt overwhelmed her. She couldn't believe she'd said those horrible things to Dad. If only she could rewind the clock a few hours and start over. If only there were something she could do . . .

Then she remembered a Bible verse she'd memorized a year ago. There *was* something she could do. *God, I'm so sorry for how I acted and what I said*, she prayed. *Please forgive me*. After school, she called Dad at work again. In tears, she apologized and asked for his forgiveness too. She hung up, feeling lighter — and free.

More to Explore: "If we confess our sins, he is faithful and just and will forgive us our sins and purify us from all unrighteousness." (1 John 1:9)

Connecting to God: "Dear God, I'm so sorry for what I did. Please forgive me and show me how to make it right to the person I hurt. Amen."

Journal Prompt: Why is forgiving yourself sometimes harder than forgiving others?

Take Action:

Everyone is human. Everyone makes honest mistakes. And sometimes, you will do wrong things, even when you know better.

Forgive yourself for the honest mistakes you make. They aren't on purpose. They are part of being human. (Forgive others — and cut others some slack — for these same things.)

Forgive yourself for wrong actions you've taken, even when you know better, like lying or gossiping about someone. Ask for forgiveness from God, then from anyone you may have hurt.

Real-girl Confession: "I detest mean people, but I can be the meanest person I know."

Indexed under: anger, divorce, guilt, rebellion, resentment

Devotion #30

"Do not worry about tomorrow, for tomorrow will worry about itself."

(Matthew 6:34)

Tied Up in Knots

Sydney's first basketball game was after school, and she was sick to her stomach with worry. She'd worked hard at practice, but she couldn't make baskets up close, let alone free throws. She had trouble passing the ball too. And once she even dribbled downcourt and shot at the opponents' basket. She could still remember how her teammates had laughed.

If I'm that bad in practice, Sydney thought, *what will I do tonight when everyone is watching?* She knew her parents and brothers would be there in the bleachers, but she wished they weren't coming. If she had to make a fool of herself, she didn't want an audience.

Halfway through the day, Sydney remembered Mom's words when she left the house that morning. "Pray for peace," Mom had said. "Trust God to help you remember what to do. And remember to have fun!"

Fun? Ha! Not possible. But at lunchtime, Sydney was too nervous to eat. So she went outside and sat by herself under a tree. It was a good place to talk to God. "Lord, help me today in my game," she whispered. "Give me the strength to shoot well and remember all the plays Coach taught us." She took a deep breath. "Help me to shrug off my mistakes and even have fun."

Sydney was calmer during the afternoon, but sometimes waves of fear washed over her again. Each time she prayed again, asking God to give her courage for the game.

Before the game, Sydney silently thanked God for helping her to do her best. At halftime she waved to her parents and grinned. With surprise, she realized she *was* having fun!

More to Explore: "God keeps your days stable and secure." (Isaiah 33:6 MSG)

Connecting to God: "Dear God, when I look at myself and my ability, I get so worried! Help me to keep my eyes on you instead—and trust you to help me do what I need to do. Amen."

Journal Prompt: Do you agree or disagree with this quote? "Courage doesn't mean that you aren't afraid. Courage means facing your fear and doing it anyway."

Take Action: Pretend your mind is a seesaw. Only one end can be up at a time. As your *trust in God* goes **up**, *fear and worry* automatically go **down**. The more you focus on trusting God, the less you worry. Time spent with God (in prayer or reading your Bible) increases your trust. Remember: Trust **up** means worry **down**.

Real-girl Confession: "I constantly worry about what others think of me. I get so flustered that I want to run and hide."

Indexed under: fear, worry

Devotion #31

"God is our refuge and strength, an ever-present help in trouble."

(Psalm 46:1)

Healing Broken Hearts

Gabriella walked in the front door, carrying her sleeping bag and backpack. Mom and Parker looked up from their game of Battleship.

"Why are *you* home?" Parker demanded. "You were supposed to stay overnight at Hailey's! Go away!"

"Parker, that's not nice," Mom said. She took the sleeping bag and put it on the couch. "But I thought you were staying at Hailey's slumber party. What happened?"

"I don't know," Gabriella said, shrugging. "Everyone was roasting hot dogs and marshmallows, and suddenly I just wanted to come home."

Mom helped Parker pick up the game. "Why don't you kids get into your pj's? It's about bedtime."

A few minutes later, Mom knocked on Gabriella's door. "Can you tell me more about what happened at Hailey's? You were looking forward to her party."

Gabriella wrapped her arms around her legs and laid her head on her knees. "I was watching Hailey's dad laughing and joking with us while we cooked over the fire, and I wanted to cry. I don't know why."

"Don't you?" Mom asked quietly.

Tears filled Gabriella's eyes. "Well, it made me remember that my own dad is gone, and he's having fun with someone else's kids now. It just makes me really sad."

"Of course it does," Mom said, hugging her. "Our smaller family makes me sad too. It's okay to feel sad. God will comfort us, and in time, he will heal your hurting heart." She handed Gabriella a tissue. "We'll get through this period. It won't last forever. I promise we'll feel happy again."

"But I want to feel better *now*."

"I understand, Gabby. I do too." Mom glanced around the bedroom. "Even though you can't see God, he's right here. He is loving you in the middle of this very hard time. He understands how you feel."

"But what do I do with the sadness?" Gabriella asked, her voice barely above a whisper.

"Tell God about it. Talk to him like you talk to me. Ask him for help and comfort as often as you need it."

Gabriella pulled up the covers as her mom turned out the light and closed the door. She took a deep breath. "Well, God," she whispered, "there's something I want to talk about with you."

More to Explore: "The eternal God is your refuge, and underneath are the everlasting arms." (Deuteronomy 33:27)

Connecting to God: "Dear God, sometimes I feel so sad I want to cry and not do anything else. But I know you're right here with me and won't ever leave me. Thank you for healing my hurts. Amen."

Journal Prompt: Why is it hard to trust God when you're hurting?

Take Action: Take positive action to help chase away sad feelings.

Read a good book. Funny books are especially helpful.

Watch a funny movie and make popcorn.

Journal your feelings — and your prayers.

Listen to music you love.

Fix a special treat, like hot chocolate with marshmallows.

Real-girl Confession: "I sit up in my room and I'm just . . . sad."

Indexed under: divorce, sadness

Devotion #32

"If someone has enough money to live well and sees a brother or sister in need but shows no compassion—how can God's love be in that person? Dear children, let's not merely say that we love each other; let us show the truth by our actions."

(1 John 3:17–18 NLT)

"Can You Give Me a Hand?"

Ava arrived at school just before the bell rang—again. Every day now, it was the same. Mom stayed in bed while Ava fed and dressed her little brothers. Her mom wasn't sick—not with something you could take medicine for, anyway. Her "sickness" came out of the bottles and cans that littered her bedroom. Since Dad died in a car accident last year, Mom's drinking had gotten much worse.

I hurt too! Ava thought. So did her little brothers. She wanted to talk to her mom about it, but somehow she just couldn't.

The house was a wreck most of the time, no meals got cooked unless Ava cooked them, and there was never enough money. Except for beer, it seemed.

Ava lied at school, telling her teachers she was fine. She couldn't tell anyone about her home life. She didn't want to embarrass Mom.

God, please have someone ask me today, Ava prayed on the way to school. *I'm hurting, and my family needs help. I need to tell somebody about what's going on at home!*

Today was the deadline to bring money for the Art Institute field trip. Ava really wanted to go, but she couldn't find any money in Mom's purse.

Ava started down the hallway to her locker, head bent and shoulders hunched. How would she survive today when she was already exhausted?

"Ava! How's it going?"

Ava glanced up. The school counselor smiled at her from her office doorway. Ava waved and kept walking. Suddenly, tears filled her eyes. She turned back to the counselor's office and said, "Well, things are bad. Do you have a minute?"

"Come on in," the counselor said. "It's okay to ask for help."

Ava found it difficult to get started. But once she did, her painful story poured out. It brought tears, but also relief.

"Ava, you don't have to struggle through feelings and problems alone," the counselor said, handing her a tissue. "You can ask for help — from God and from people."

"Okay." Ava wiped her eyes and smiled. "Thanks for caring."

More to Explore: "Carry each other's burdens, and in this way you will fulfill the law of Christ." (Galatians 6:2)

Connecting to God: "Dear God, sometimes I feel like I can't keep going. Please help me, and give me courage to be honest and ask others for help. Amen."

Journal Prompt: Sometimes, it is hard to talk to our parents even when we want to. Write a letter telling your mom or dad something you are too uncomfortable to say out loud. Consider giving them the letter.

Take Action: *It is healthy to ask for help,* when help is what we need.

Things you might ask for:

> information
>
> a hug
>
> someone to listen
>
> prayer
>
> a ride

Real-girl Confession: "I'm really angry about having to pick up the slack for my parents."

Indexed under: alcoholism, death, honesty, overloaded

Devotion #33

"[God] will not crush the weakest reed or put out a flickering candle. He will bring justice to all who have been wronged."

(Isaiah 42:3 NLT)

Help for the Weak

Shae only had one close friend, Alyssa. But Alyssa had tons of friends. If Shae couldn't go somewhere, Alyssa simply found someone else who could. Shae hated being left out, so she went wherever Alyssa wanted to go—usually the mall.

One Saturday in an accessories shop, Shae was trying on headbands when Alyssa clutched her arm. "I'm bored. Let's get a pizza." Then, she dragged Shae out of the store.

Seconds later, Shae was horrified when a security guard grabbed both girls by the arms. "Come with me, ladies," he said.

Alyssa had shoplifted two bracelets. Because the girls were together, Shae was held for questioning too. Shae was so ashamed, even though she hadn't stolen anything. She prayed desperately for help while waiting to be questioned by the manager.

An hour later, Shae's dad picked her up. That night, her parents told her she couldn't be friends with Alyssa anymore. Shae understood why, but she felt hopeless just the same. "I need friends! If God is love and God is good," she said, "then why didn't he stop this from happening?"

"That's a question everyone asks sometimes," Dad said. "God is all-powerful, so he can do anything. He's also all-loving, and all his decisions are good—even if the things that happen don't *feel* good at the time."

Mom nodded. "After you come through a tough time, you'll often see the good God brought from it."

Tears welled up in Shae's eyes. "How could any good come from being accused of shoplifting?" she cried.

"After you are calmer, you may see several good things," Dad said. "The guard believed you, so you weren't arrested. That's one good thing. And you discovered an important truth about your friend's character."

"And that's good?" Shae asked.

"You can try to help your friends," Dad said, "but at some point it's important to ask yourself if you really want a friend like that. Do you really want to hang around with a person who leads you into trouble?"

Mom moved to sit on the couch next to Shae. "Other good things often come out of these hard times," she said. "I can think of three.

You'll trust God even more! He often uses hard times to draw us closer to him as we spend time in prayer.

You'll learn that God is faithful. The next time you have a problem, you'll remember how God brought you through this time—and you'll trust him to do it again.

And you'll learn from your mistakes so you won't repeat them. God knows that sometimes we need to suffer consequences for a bad choice so we'll learn not to do it again."

Dad took Shae's hand. "You need to know one more thing about God. He understands that you're human, and that you're weak. We *all* are weak in some area. He just wants to help you when you're weak—and make you strong."

Shae did pray and ask God to make her strong. She also asked him for a new friend. Even though it was hard, she waited for God to answer her prayers. Eventually Shae made friends with a girl much more like her. And she learned she could trust God during hard times.

More to Explore: "I have prayed for you ... that your faith may not fail." (Luke 22:32)

Connecting to God: "Dear God, I'm sorry for doing something I know is wrong. Help me be stronger next time and make a good choice. Amen."

Journal Prompt: Some excuses I make for my behavior include...

Take Action: If someone asks you to do something you're uncomfortable with, say no. Here are some good ways to do it:

Say no repeatedly and firmly.

Walk away quickly and don't look back.

Ignore the question and talk to someone else.

Real-girl Confession: "I just wanted to fit in."

Indexed under: friendship, peer pressure

Devotion #34

"God sets the lonely in families."

(Psalm 68:6)

"I'm Not Alone"

Madeline, her dad, and her older brother were at the school's annual fund-raiser game night. They played mini golf, tossed rings at a fake cactus, and then threw water balloons. They ate caramel apples and funnel cake until they were stuffed. Madeline forgot about the divorce all evening—until the photographer asked them to dress up in Western clothes and pose for a family picture.

"We can't have a family picture!" Madeline protested. "We aren't a family anymore!" In tears, she turned to run out of the gym.

Madeline's older brother grabbed her arm, his face red with embarrassment. "Sorry about that," he said to the photographer. "Our mom moved out. We don't have a family anymore."

"I want to go home," Madeline said, heading for the door.

In the car, Dad turned around and looked at Madeline and her brother in the backseat. "I have to say that I'm shocked to hear that you think we aren't a family any longer. We're *still* a family. Our family has just changed."

Madeline shook her head. "How can we be a family when we don't have a mom anymore? I miss her so much!"

"You still have a mother, even though she doesn't live with us," Dad said. "I miss her too." He rubbed his face and then smiled. "Our family is different now, but we're still a family. We'll keep on loving and taking care of each other."

"But our family isn't the same anymore," Madeline said quietly. "It's lonely when families change."

Dad nodded. "Maybe it's time we saw more of our other family members," he said. "We haven't seen your grandparents or aunts and uncles for a while. That would help us with the loneliness."

Madeline's brother snapped on his seat belt. "And we could sign up for family camp at church. We had fun there last year."

"Good thinking!" Dad said. "Spending more time with our church family is a great idea. The Bible talks about having friends who help you when you're down. And we'll continue to pray for your mom. Even if she doesn't live here, she's still an important part of the family."

One other thing they did was visit the dog pound. They brought home a new black Lab puppy. They bought wood for a doghouse and built it together. Madeline painted it, and they all helped train the puppy.

"Our family changed again," Madeline said, realizing some changes could be good. Now whenever she was lonely, she also had a dog to hug!

More to Explore: "If either of them falls down, one can help the other up. But pity anyone who falls and has no one to help them up!" (Ecclesiastes 4:10)

Connecting to God: "Dear God, sometimes I feel so lonely that my heart hurts. Please comfort me and help me to feel your presence with me at all times. Amen."

Journal Prompt: Five fun things you can do when you're alone are . . .

Take Action: Advice from real kids on how to deal with loneliness . . .

"Take a cool toy or game to school, and if someone asks to play with you, say yes. They might ask you to play with them next time."

"Listen to music, or learn to play an instrument."

"Go for a walk or a bike ride."

"Join a club at school or near where you live."

"Help a parent do a job. You'll have someone to talk to, and then you'll know how to do things when you're grown up."

Real-girl Confession: "I try to talk to my mom, but she doesn't understand."

Indexed under: change, divorce, loneliness

Devotion #35

"He has sent me to comfort the brokenhearted and to proclaim that captives will be released and prisoners will be freed."

(Isaiah 61:1 NLT)

Shh! It's a Secret!

Mrs. Foley, the school counselor, stood in front of the classroom. "Attention, girls," she said, clapping her hands. "The film you're about to see is about secrets: good secrets and harmful secrets."

Elise tensed up. She gripped her hands together in her lap and stared straight ahead.

"Secrets are such fun!" Mrs. Foley said. "We keep secrets before Christmas, wanting our gifts to be a surprise. We have dreams and goals for our lives, and we only share those secrets with our best friends. Those are great secrets!"

The counselor paused and looked around the classroom. Elise's heart hammered as Mrs. Foley's gaze passed over her.

Mrs. Foley continued, "However, not all secrets are good. In fact, sometimes it is a very bad idea to keep something a secret. Some secrets are so harmful that they can make you sick."

Elise held her breath. Did Mrs. Foley somehow know her secret?

"Let's watch the film now, and we'll discuss it afterward."

In the opening segment, a fifth-grader named Chloe talked about her older sister. "My parents don't know that my sister goes to parties where she drinks a lot of alcohol. She doesn't want to get into trouble, so she begs me to keep it a secret." Chloe pauses and swallows hard. "I don't sleep well anymore. I'm worried about my sister's dangerous behavior—and about what Dad will do if he catches her."

The next segment showed a sixth-grader named Lauren who babysat for her neighbors during summer vacation. Her neighbors, Mr. and Mrs. Jones, both worked. "The job paid pretty well," Lauren admitted, "but there were so many things I needed for school! One day, I spotted a jar full of change in a kitchen cupboard. I only took a few quarters at a time, but over the summer I stole more than twenty-five dollars." She hung her head. "My stomach hurts a lot these days, especially when I see my neighbors."

Mrs. Foley then talked about the freedom and peace that resulted if harmful secrets were told to a trusted adult. She invited anyone who needed to talk to come to her office at any time.

Long after the video was over and they'd gone back to study hall, Elise thought about what Mrs. Foley had said. It sounded like something her mother had told her just last week when she'd asked Elise why she seemed depressed lately. "The Bible says Jesus came to set the prisoners free," she'd said. "Things we are afraid to talk about can make us captives, but God wants us to be free."

Elise's secret was different from what she'd seen in the video. Their nice neighbor, Jack, brought Elise candy sometimes. Then, when no one was around, he kissed her. Elise hated it. Jack said he wouldn't hurt her, but he touched her in private places. Elise knew it wasn't right—no matter what Jack said. But she'd been afraid to tell anyone. Until now.

She headed to Mrs. Foley's office right after school. Telling the truth was going to be hard, but it would set her free. She had God's word on that.

More to Explore: "Jesus said, 'If you hold to my teaching, you are really my disciples. Then you will know the truth, and the truth will set you free.'" (John 8:31–32)

Connecting to God: "Dear God, I'm so worried about the secret I'm keeping. I need to tell someone I can trust. Show me whom to talk to — and give me courage to tell the truth. Amen."

Journal Prompt: Can there be a connection between headaches or stomachaches and a secret you aren't talking about?

Take Action: Don't keep harmful secrets. List some adults you trust — and can talk to . . .

1. _____

2. _____

3. _____

Real-girl Confession: "I'm afraid I'll be punished if I tell."

Indexed under: abuse/sexual, secrets

Devotion #36

"We are confident that he hears us whenever we ask for anything that pleases him."

(1 John 5:14 NLT)

Dad Wouldn't Steal!

Jenna couldn't believe what had happened. One day, they were enjoying their home with a pool, laughing at the dinner table, and planning their summer vacation. The next day, Dad was arrested and taken to jail—in handcuffs! Police came to their front door, said some things Jenna didn't understand, and then led Dad to the police car. Jenna thought her knees would buckle.

"Mom, what happened?" Jenna cried.

"I'm in shock too." Mom led Jenna to the couch. "The police officer said the company Dad works for is missing a lot of money."

"Dad wouldn't steal it!"

"There must be some mistake," Mom agreed. "I'll call our lawyer right away."

It turned out that the charges were true. Dad had stolen money from the company he worked for, and he would probably go to prison.

Jenna was too shocked for days to think clearly. She was a jumble of feelings: confusion, fear, anger, and disappointment. How could Dad have done that? She prayed for God to keep her dad out of prison. How could he survive that? After praying for a week, it still looked as if Dad was going to prison.

"I told God what we need," Jenna explained to Mom, "but nothing's changed. I've prayed and prayed, so why doesn't God answer?"

Jenna's mom pulled her close. "God always answers, and he gives the answer we most need. It isn't always what we want to hear."

Jenna shook her head. "Then prayer doesn't work. I'm quitting."

Mom rested her chin on top of Jenna's head. "God promises to give us what is best. He might decide that it would be best for Dad to learn a hard lesson from all this. We will have to wait and see. But God always hears our cries for help."

Jenna didn't get what she wanted. Her dad did end up going to prison. During the months he was away, they had to sell the house and move to a smaller home. But they were content with the smaller house, especially when Dad finally came home.

"It was a hard way to learn about the consequences of greed, but it was good for me," he said after he had served his sentence.

Although they no longer owned the fancy house with the pool, Jenna was grateful to have her family together again—an answer to her prayer.

More to Explore: "If you don't know what you're doing, pray to the Father. He loves to help. You'll get his help ..." (James 1:5 MSG)

Connecting to God: "Dear God, this problem is more than I can handle! I'm shocked and confused and don't know where to turn. Please, help me! I love you and trust that you will do the best thing in this situation. Amen."

Journal Prompt: Write about any anger you feel that makes it difficult to forgive a parent or other adult in your life.

Take Action: *If you have a parent in prison, don't be afraid to ask questions.*

> Can I call my mom or dad? (Not always, but they will treasure a letter, drawing, or photos from you.)
>
> Do my parents still love me? (You are still loved by your parent, no matter where you happen to be living right now — or with whom.)
>
> Is this my fault? (No, it is not your fault. Your parent did something wrong and is experiencing the consequences. You could not have prevented it.)
>
> Can I do something to help? (Write often. Pray for help to forgive your parent.)

Real-girl Confession: "You feel like you're the only one."

Indexed under: anger, confusion, disappointment, fear

Devotion #37

"The rain came down, the streams rose, and the winds blew and beat against that house; yet it did not fall, because it had its foundation on the rock."

(Matthew 7:25)

When Bad Things Happen

Savannah's assignment for current events was to report on something happening in the country or the world each day for two weeks. She had to find her information in the daily newspaper or on a TV news show. Savannah thought it was an interesting assignment. She'd love to learn about what was happening around the globe.

She only enjoyed it for about fifteen minutes. But as Savannah watched the evening news with her dad, she realized much of the world isn't like her safe and secure home. Her family wasn't rich, but they were comfortable. Savannah had everything she needed and many things she wanted.

Savannah learned from her current events assignment that this wasn't true for many people in the world. Many had lost their jobs and their homes. Diseases in foreign countries killed thousands of people. Children in many lands were hungry, and some were starving to death. People were getting killed in shootings and earthquakes and hurricanes and wars. Savannah worried every night and often had nightmares.

One evening at bedtime, Savannah asked her mother, "What will we do if Dad loses his job? Or an earthquake destroys our house?" She swallowed hard. "What if you get sick and die? Bad things are happening everywhere!"

Mom held Savannah close. "Yes, bad things happen all over the world. Hard times sooner or later come to everyone." She looked Savannah in the eye. "Tough times help us remember how much we need God. When bad things happen, we'll depend on him, not on our jobs or health."

"Aren't you afraid, Mom? How can you be so calm about it?"

Mom smiled. "I've been through some tough times. I've seen that the Bible is true when it promises that God will comfort us and provide for us. I've learned that when I build my life on following the teachings of Jesus, no storm can shake me for long. As you go through more experiences, you'll discover that too."

Savannah took a deep breath and smiled. What her mom said made sense. After they prayed together, Savannah fell peacefully asleep.

More to Explore: "All of creation will be shaken and removed, so that only unshakable things will remain." (Hebrews 12:27 NLT)

Connecting to God: "Dear God, when I see what's happening in the world, I get scared. Help me to keep my focus on you instead — and trust you to take care of me. Amen."

Journal Prompt: What keeps you stuck thinking about a fearful event?

Take Action: *Whether your worries are big or small, you can take these steps:*

1. Try to figure out what you're worried about.
2. Pray (or journal your prayers), and tell God all of your fears.

3. Memorize a favorite scripture to fight fear (2 Timothy 1:7 is a good one!).

4. Ask for help from an adult you trust.

5. Think about ways to make the situation better — and take action.

Real-girl Confession: "I try to forget, but the worry takes over."

Indexed under: fear, worry

Devotion #38

"A person without self-control is like a house with its doors and windows knocked out."

(Proverbs 25:28 MSG)

Feelings Don't Get to Choose

Olivia's dad was out of work for six months before he found another good job in a town two states away. He'd moved and started his new job a month ago. Olivia and Mom would join him when their house was sold. Even so, Olivia couldn't shake the feeling of sadness since her dad left.

She doodled on her math worksheet and then stared out the window, wishing it were time for lunch. Sighing, she finally closed her math book with the unfinished worksheet folded inside it. How could she do homework when she felt this sad?

In the lunchroom, Olivia overheard two of her friends ahead of her in line.

"Olivia's dad moved out," the first friend said.

"He probably has a girlfriend," the second friend said. "I bet her parents are getting a divorce."

Olivia was so furious at the lies that she walked up to the second girl and slapped her. The girl screamed, and the lunchroom monitor pulled Olivia away and marched her to the principal's office. The principal talked to Olivia about her actions, then called Olivia's mother.

After school, over hot chocolate and a donut, Olivia and her mom talked about what had happened. After calming down, Olivia felt horribly embarrassed.

"I was just so mad when I heard them!" Olivia stormed. "Dad has a new job, but instead they said he left us because he has a girlfriend!"

Mom pressed her lips together for a moment. "Frankly, that makes me angry too," she said, "but it's times like this when you need self-control. Do you know what that is?"

Olivia sighed. "I remember that 'fruit of the Spirit' song we sang in Bible school a few years ago. Self-control is in that list."

"Exactly." Mom put another handful of marshmallows in her hot chocolate. "Self-control is a fruit of the Holy Spirit working inside a person who has accepted Jesus as Savior. Self-control is just what it sounds like: controlling yourself."

"Which is what I didn't do today," Olivia admitted.

"I'm afraid so." Mom sipped her cocoa. "With self-control, you can choose a godly action or godly words instead of lashing out at people without thinking."

"I know," Olivia said, her head hanging. "I just can't seem to make myself do the right thing."

"Nobody can, at least not for long," Mom said. "I can't either."

Olivia's head snapped up. "Yes, you do! All the time!"

"No, I don't do things right by myself either," Mom said. "I have to ask for the Holy Spirit's help to do the right thing."

"Even so, what do you do with your feelings?" Olivia asked, remembering her rage in the lunchroom.

"I'm not telling you to ignore your feelings — not at all," Mom said. "But paying attention to your feelings doesn't mean your feelings get to decide your actions. You mustn't say, 'I'm really mad, so I'm going to knock you down.'"

Olivia pulled her math book from her school bag. "I guess I have to do my math problems too, even though I don't *feel* like it."

Mom laughed and nodded. "I'm afraid so. But self-control will help you be more successful—like when you get a good grade for doing your homework. You'll also be happier because you'll keep your friends. Self-control will help you handle tough situations much better, in ways that please God."

More to Explore: "Better to have self-control than to conquer a city." (Proverbs 16:32 NLT)

Connecting to God: "Dear God, sometimes I just want to do whatever I feel like, even if it is a poor decision. Help me to choose the right actions. And please help me to follow through on them. Amen."

Journal Prompt: Does being tired (or hungry, or lonely) make your emotions harder to control? If so, what can you do about it?

Take Action: Warning signs that you might erupt!

Are you breathing faster?

Is your face getting red?

Are your muscles tense or your fists clenched tight?

Do you feel like yelling?

Do you want to break something or hit someone?

Do you have a headache or stomachache or want to cry? (Some people bury anger *inside*.)

Real-girl Confession: "Sometimes, I just want to scream or throw things!"

Indexed under: anger, gossip, sadness

Devotion #39

"Two are better off than one, because together they can work more effectively.

(Ecclesiastes 4:9 GNT)

Many Hands Make Light Work

"Mom, you have to come watch this movie," Karly called. "It's really good."

"And make some popcorn too!" her little brother James shouted.

"In a minute," Mom answered from the kitchen.

"You're missing the best part!" Karly paused the DVD and headed to the kitchen. "What are you doing?" Karly and James had already finished cleaning the supper dishes.

"Making tuna salad for lunches, plus a casserole to freeze for next week. It helps to work ahead," Mom said, rinsing her hands. "I'll be done pretty soon. I just need to throw in a load of laundry before I sit down."

"Then can you watch with us?" Karly asked. They used to watch movies on Friday nights as a whole family, but ever since Dad left, Mom never had free time anymore. She worked at an office now, then came home and cleaned and grocery shopped and did laundry. "You never have time to sit down with us anymore."

James grabbed his mom's hand. "I'll do the laundry for you. You can sit down."

Mom laughed, and then sighed. "I *am* awfully tired, but I'll do it."

"James is right though," Karly said. "We do dishes and clean our rooms like always. But we can help more if you'd tell us what to do."

Mom's shoulders slumped. "Thank you, kids. I thought I could do it all myself, but I can see that it's not working. I miss having time for fun with you both." She smiled. "I guess the Bible is right. Working together is more effective than working alone. My grandma used to say that 'many hands make light work.'"

Karly grabbed a pen and notepad. They sat down at the kitchen table to make a list of all the chores that had to be done to run the house.

"Let's pray first," Mom said, taking their hands. "With God's help — and with each other — we can do this!"

Over the next half hour, Karly and James each made a checklist for the extra chores they would do. Mom also decided to teach them how to cook simple, healthful meals on the weekends.

Helping each other and sharing chores gave Mom more free time. She decided on a household project to do together as a family. They cleaned out one of the closets, painted it yellow and orange, then turned it into a clubhouse. Now, sometimes on Friday nights, they picnic in their clubhouse!

More to Explore: "Though one may be overpowered, two can defend themselves. A cord of three strands is not quickly broken." (Ecclesiastes 4:12)

Connecting to God: "Dear God, thank you for my parent who works so hard. Help me to be a caring member of my family. Amen."

Journal Prompt: How could you make doing chores more fun? For example, you might put on music or plan a reward when finished.

Take Action: Get organized! Chores can feel overwhelming until you get a system. Try using one of these:

A clipboard with a list

To-do list on the computer

Chore chart on the refrigerator

Tiny notebook for your pocket

Real-girl Confession: "My grandma says that 'many hands make light work.' She's right!"

Indexed under: change, divorce

Devotion #40

"Do everything without grumbling or arguing."

(Philippians 2:14)

The Danger of Complaining

Mariah was excited that her mom was expecting twins — until they arrived. The baby boys cried for hours, day and night, in the nursery across the hall. It was impossible to get any sleep. Grandma moved in for a while to help out and was staying in Mariah's bedroom. Mariah was already tired of sleeping on an air mattress.

"Don't get me wrong," Mariah told her best friend, Kayla. "I love baby Jonah and Josiah. But it's a zoo around here now! People stop in to bring food and presents for the babies, and just hang around forever." Everyone wanted to hold the babies and take pictures of the babies.

"At least your grandma's staying with you. You always talk about having fun doing stuff with her."

"I *used* to! But now Grandma's always busy feeding or changing diapers or burping the babies," Mariah complained. "She and I haven't done one single fun thing since she came."

Kayla tilted her head to one side. "Is there *anything* you like about the twins? You sound like you're sorry they were born."

Mariah's head snapped up. "What?" Did she really sound like that?

Kayla touched Mariah's arm. "I don't mean to sound like I'm preaching at you, but remember the Sunday school lesson last week? How the Israelites were grumbling and complaining, and so they didn't get into the Promised Land?"

Mariah nodded and took a deep breath. "I know complaining is wrong. It's kind of funny, but I don't even like to be around people who complain all the time. I need to stop it."

"It's okay to tell me how you feel," Kayla said. "That's what best friends are for. But maybe you can think of some positive things about the twins too."

Mariah nodded. "I guess I was feeling sorry for myself. And yes, there are lots of things I love about the babies." She showed Kayla how Jonah grabbed her finger and held on tight. Then she cuddled Josiah on her shoulder, loving the warm snuggly feeling. "Remember how our teacher also said that going on and on about your bad feelings can actually make you feel *worse*? I don't want that."

Kayla smiled. "That's probably one of the reasons God tells us not to do it."

Mariah laughed. "You're right. Here." She handed Josiah to her friend. "Here, have a baby."

More to Explore: "Don't grumble about each other, brothers and sisters, or you will be judged." (James 5:9 NLT)

Connecting to God: "Dear God, I'm tempted to complain when things don't go my way. Help me to stop grumbling and thank you for things in my life instead. Help me to say how I honestly feel, but then focus on something I'm grateful for. Amen."

Journal Prompt: What do you think about this anonymous quote? "If you took one-tenth the energy you put into complaining and applied it to solving the problem, you'd be surprised by how well things can work out ..."

Take Action: We all want to tell someone how we feel, but talking about our situation over and over can easily change into complaining, which is *not* helpful. If you or a friend have gone from sharing to complaining, try these statements...

"What ideas do you have that could help in this situation?"

"It sounds like you're actually feeling [afraid, angry, let down, betrayed]."

"Let's pray and ask God to show you something good about this."

"Is there anything I can do to help?"

Real-girl Confession: "Sometimes, I just have to get things off my chest!"

Indexed under: complaining

Devotion #41

"I can do all this through him who gives me strength."

(Philippians 4:13 NIV)

Nothing's Ever Going to Change!

Katelyn was so angry. She needed track shoes, and Dad had promised that tonight he'd take her shopping. But on the way home, she'd seen his car parked at his favorite bar. He was spending his paycheck on alcohol. Again. There wouldn't be any money left for a shopping trip.

Totally frustrated, Katelyn kicked at the gravel in the driveway. She was so mad! She brushed away the tears brimming in her eyes. She felt so helpless, and there wasn't anything she could do about it.

She climbed the porch stairs, took one look at a wilted potted plant, and kicked it down the cement steps. The pot smashed to pieces. Then Katelyn threw her books down. She hated her life. "Things are never going to change!" she yelled.

Katelyn plopped down on the top step and leaned her chin in her hand. She felt so trapped by her dad's drinking—and the constant money shortage. At this rate, Katelyn was never going to have the things she needed.

"You all right?" called a frail voice.

Katelyn peered around the corner of the porch. Mrs. Miller was pulling weeds in her flower garden. Katelyn cringed. She liked Mrs. Miller. She'd gone to church with her a few times, and Mrs. Miller had even bought her a Bible. She hoped the old lady hadn't seen her kick the pot and break it.

"I'm fine," Katelyn called back.

Mrs. Miller came over, leaning on her cane, and sat down beside Katelyn. "Wow!" she said. "Looks like that pot exploded."

"It did," Katelyn said, "with a little help from my foot."

"Something happen with your dad?"

Katelyn sighed. "We were supposed to shop for new shoes for me tonight because he got paid today." She pounded one fist into the palm of her other hand. "I just walked past the bar, and his car is there. There goes our money—again."

"I'm sorry, honey." Mrs. Miller patted her hand. "Your dad might change some day, or he might not. It's not your job to fix the adults in your life."

"But I feel so helpless!" Katelyn said. "I'm sick and tired of getting my hopes up, then have him smash them. I love my dad, but I hate his drinking."

"You sound worn out, dear," Mrs. Miller said.

"I am. Worn out. Exhausted. Pooped. Bushed." Katelyn tried to smile. "It's just that this could go on until I graduate from high school. I don't think I can take six more years of this. I haven't got the strength."

Mrs. Miller patted Katelyn's knee. "Remember when we talked about being able to draw on God's strength?"

Katelyn nodded. "You said that after I accepted Jesus as my Savior that I could ask God to help me." She shook her head. "To be honest, I don't ever remember to ask God for help. I'm used to taking care of myself instead."

"I know," Mrs. Miller said, "and I'm sorry your life is like that. But God wants to help you and give you strength to live a good life, despite your dad's drinking problem."

Katelyn wished she could believe that. "You don't suppose God has some extra track shoes, do you?" she asked.

"Let's ask, shall we?" Mrs. Miller said, taking Katelyn's hand. Briefly she prayed and asked God to show how Katelyn could get some new shoes.

That weekend, Mrs. Miller introduced Katelyn to some families at church and explained about her babysitting services. Soon, she had plenty of babysitting jobs. She remembered to pray for God's strength every day. Within a few weeks, Katelyn had earned enough money to buy her own track shoes.

More to Explore: "Be strong in the Lord and in his mighty power." (Ephesians 6:10)

Connecting to God: "Dear God, life has been hard for so long! Please, fill me with your strength and show me how to make positive changes in my life. Amen."

Journal Prompt: Children of alcoholics are often afraid and sad. What do you do when these feelings overtake you?

Take Action: Katelyn did many things to help herself deal with living with an alcoholic:

> She talked about her problem to a close friend.
>
> She admitted her confused feelings, how she loved her dad but hated his drinking.
>
> She was involved in an enjoyable activity at school.
>
> She trusted God to meet her needs and give her strength.
>
> She found an AlaTeen group to join, where she could share her feelings with other kids in this situation (see the Resource Section at the end.)

Real-girl Confession: "Neglect is my life."

Indexed under: alcoholism, anger, needs

Devotion #42

"We aren't fighting against human enemies but against . . . spiritual powers of evil in the heavens."

(Ephesians 6:12 CEB)

At War With the Enemy

"Do I have to go in there?" Daniella asked her mom. The bright smiley face and Bible verse on the door didn't fool her. The last place she expected to find smiling people was a recovery group for kids.

"Yes, I really think it would help," Mom said. "Talking to other kids with the same problem will make you feel better."

"This is so unfair!" Daniella clenched her fists. "Dad's the one with the drinking problem. Why do *I* have to get help?"

"Because whether we like it or not, his drinking makes things hard for us too," Mom said. "My women's group helps me. Please try this, at least once or twice."

Daniella glanced at her mother. Sometimes she hated her dad, but she didn't want to add to Mom's problems. She took a deep breath and reached for the doorknob. At least the meeting wasn't at her own church. Hopefully, she wouldn't know anyone there. "Okay, see you later."

At first, Daniella stared at her lap while other kids talked. But as they went around the circle, sharing stories, she gradually relaxed. There was no need to be embarrassed. Most of these kids were sharing stories just like her own.

One girl's voice was so low she could hardly be heard. "We find my dad asleep at the kitchen table when we get up to go to school in the morning," she said. "We have to be really quiet, and we skip breakfast so we don't wake him up."

The biggest boy, Juan, cracked his knuckles while he talked. "I have a lot of scary times with my dad. Once I found him lying outside in the snow in the middle of winter. He had come home from the bar late at night, and he fell. I thought he was dead."

Another girl, who didn't give her name, sat with her hands folded in her lap and stared over the top of Daniella's head. "Sometimes, I just want to take care of Mom, make her something to eat, or help her get out of her work uniform. But she gets mad and swears and chases me away. I don't know how to help her."

Miss Bender, the leader, turned to Daniella. "We're so glad you could come today. Would you be willing to share an experience with us?"

Daniella looked at the other kids. None of them seemed glad to be there, but their stories had somehow helped her. She wasn't alone like she had believed. Maybe her story would help one of them.

She took a deep breath and stared at her shoes. "One time, Dad left me and my friend at home on a Friday night while he went out. Mom was working. Dad didn't come home, so we went to my friend's house. Her mom was real nice about it. My dad didn't pick me up at my friend's house until Saturday morning. He was hung over. He didn't talk at all on the ride home, and he went to bed as soon as we got home. The next day, he acted like nothing had happened." She brushed tears away and looked up. "That day was my birthday. He never even mentioned it."

Miss Bender nodded in sympathy. "Thank you — all of

you—for sharing. Our time is up now. Remember that your parents are *not* the real enemy. Let's pray now."

When she was leaving, Daniella turned back to the leader. "See you next week," she said.

More to Explore: "Never stop praying, especially for others. Always pray by the power of the Spirit." (Ephesians 6:18 CEV)

Connecting to God: "Dear God, thank you for showing me I'm not alone with my problem. There are others who can understand and pray with me. Please help my parent to be set free from the drinking problem. Amen."

Journal Prompt: Write a letter to your parent who drinks too much about how you feel. You do not need to send it.

Take Action: Do *not* ride in a car with a driver who has been drinking. It is not safe. Walk, or get a ride with a trusted adult who has not been drinking. If you find yourself in a car with a driver before you realize he or she has been drinking, sit in the middle of the backseat. Lock your doors, and secure your safety belt. Pray all the way home, and stay calm.

Real-girl Confession: "I mostly just remember always feeling afraid 24/7."

Indexed under: alcoholism, honesty

Devotion #43

"Don't insist on getting even; that's not for you to do. 'I'll do the judging,' says God. 'I'll take care of it.'"

(Romans 12:19 MSG)

It Just Isn't Fair

Georgia tried hard to hold back her tears, but her broken legs hurt so much. She was in two casts up to her hips since the accident. She'd been crossing the street when a teen driver came roaring around the corner while talking on his phone. Georgia didn't think he even saw her before hitting her.

Mom and Dad had just come to visit, and Georgia tried to be brave for them.

Dad took her hand and squeezed. "I'm afraid we have some disturbing news."

Georgia's heart began to race. "What? Did the doctors tell you something? Am I going to be crippled?"

"No!" Mom said. "Nothing like that. We have every reason to believe you will heal just fine."

Dad nodded. "Your mom's right. But the news is about the young man who struck you."

"I bet he feels really guilty," Georgia said. "I thought he might come and see how I'm doing."

"Deep down, he probably does feel horrified at what happened," Dad said, "but he's handling the guilt by lying."

"Lying about what?" Georgia asked.

"He claims you darted out from between parked cars right into his path," Mom said. "He says you're to blame for the accident."

"That's a lie!" The tears ran down Georgia's cheeks. "It's so unfair!" she cried.

Dad nodded. "You're right. You certainly don't deserve the pain you're in. Life isn't fair, but God is just and fair. With his help, we can forgive the person instead of trying to hurt him back."

"I don't want that." Georgia pounded her fist on the blanket. "He deserves to be the one in pain! I wish I could pay him back!"

Mom rubbed Georgia's clenched fist. "Wanting to get even is tempting, but God cautions against taking revenge. Instead, we need to let him take care of the situation."

"But that's not right," Georgia cried.

"It's not over yet," Dad assured. "When you give the unfair situation to God, you can trust him to make things right. He will make sure justice is done, in his own way, in his own good time. Let's give it to God and pray for the truth to come out."

Mom pointed at the bouquets of flowers around the room. "Focus on what's good about your life instead of the rotten thing that happened."

It was very hard at first, but Georgia did just that. She focused on the gifts and flowers from friends. And when she went back to school on crutches, she enjoyed the extra attention at school. Soon, she was back into the school routine and focusing forward.

More to Explore: "I will take revenge; I will pay them back. In due time, their feet will slip. Their day of disaster will arrive." (Deuteronomy 32:35 NLT)

Connecting to God: "Dear God, I'm so angry and hurt about what happened to me. Help me to forgive this person and move on with my life. I trust you to make things right someday. Amen."

Journal Prompt: What does this anonymous quote mean to you? "Life is never fair, and perhaps it is a good thing for most of us that it is not." [Hint: Aren't you glad that you don't *always* get what you deserve?]

Take Action: When you're tempted to focus on the unfair thing that happened to you, try saying these statements out loud:

"Life doesn't always seem fair, but it's still good."

"Life is too precious to waste time hating anyone."

"This difficult time will pass."

"I won't always feel like this."

"This event is a small part of my life."

"I choose to focus on the good things."

"I can't compare my life to others."

"I have no idea what others are going through."

"In one year, will this matter?"

"God is still in control, loves me, and is working things out for my good."

Real-girl Confession: "Talk about unfair! I'm so mad I could spit nails!"

Indexed under: anger, revenge

Devotion #44

"You shall not circulate a false report."

(Exodus 23:1 NKJV)

A Narrow Escape

Viviana was peering into the refrigerator, trying to decide what to fix for lunch, when the front doorbell rang. Her mom wasn't home from work yet. Viviana followed the house rule of looking through the peephole before opening the door. It was just her neighbor, Marvin. Sometimes, he trimmed their bushes or fixed leaks on their roof.

Viviana opened the door. "Hi, Marvin. Sorry, but Mom's not home yet."

"I know," he said, a worried look on his face. "She just called me."

"She called *you?* But why?" Viviana asked, upset by her neighbor's anxious expression.

Marvin rattled his car keys. "She got really sick at work, and she wants me to pick her up. She wants you to come with me."

Viviana pushed her feet into her tennis shoes and didn't stop to tie them. "Why does she want me to come with you?"

"She said she wanted me to take you both to your grandma's house for the rest of the day. And she said for you to bring your homework with you."

Viviana smiled at that. "Trust Mom to remember my home-work even when she's sick." She picked up her school bag that was still by the door. She started to follow Marvin. "Wait a second. I forgot something." She ran back to her bedroom for a book and to feed her fish.

"Hurry up!" Marvin called. He came down the hall, grasped Viviana's arm and pulled her along. "We don't have any time to waste."

Viviana was climbing into Marvin's backseat when she glanced down the street. "Hey, that's Mom's car! She must be better."

Marvin brushed his hair back, looking panicky. "Um, yes, well ..."

Mom pulled into the driveway and jumped out of her car. "Where are you going?" she demanded.

Puzzled because Mom looked perfectly healthy, Viviana climbed back out of Marvin's car. "Marvin said you were sick and he's taking us to Grandma's house."

Mom pulled Viviana close to her. "Marvin lied to you. I'm not sick, and I never called him." She pointed a finger at Marvin. "Get away from us right now."

Marvin left, and the first thing Mom did when they got inside was lock the door, and then she called the police. Viviana sat on the couch, shaking. She'd had a narrow escape. She didn't know what Marvin had planned to do, but it looked like he meant to hurt her. *Thank you, God, for protecting me!* she prayed.

More to Explore: "A false witness will not go unpunished, nor will a liar escape." (Proverbs 19:5 NLT)

Connecting to God: "Dear God, I know that you never lie, but sometimes people do. It's very scary to realize this. Protect me from lying people who want to harm me. Help the truth to come out! Amen."

Journal Prompt: If a neighbor or relative says or does something that makes you uncomfortable, what are some things you could do?

Take Action: You are walking home from the mall, and it starts to rain hard. You don't have an umbrella or raincoat. A car pulls up to the curb, and a woman asks if you'd like a ride. You know you're not supposed to talk to strangers, but you're getting soaked and the smiling lady sounds really nice. What should you do?

1. Stay away from the car. Stay on the sidewalk and call your answer to her.
2. Say "No, thank you." If the lady offers again, say "No!"
3. Tell your parent or guardian or a trusted adult as soon as you get home.
4. All of the above.

Real-girl Confession: "I couldn't stop shaking after it happened."

Devotion #45

> " 'For I know the plans I have for you,' declares the LORD, 'plans to prosper you and not to harm you, plans to give you hope and a future.' "

> (Jeremiah 29:11)

I Want to Decide!

Lydia stood on the front porch and watched as neighbors and strangers touched her personal belongings for sale. After the divorce, Mom said they couldn't afford to stay in their house. Many of their things had to be sold. Mom said many of their stuffed animals, outgrown clothes, and toys needed to go. An apartment would be too small to store it all.

"Why do *you* get to decide that we have to move?" Lydia had asked. "It's our house too! Why don't Ellie and I get to vote?"

"It's a grown-up decision," Mom had said. "I know how much money I make in my job, and I know this part of town is too expensive. I'll give you choices whenever I can, but this decision is mine."

That night Lydia joined her mom at the kitchen table while Mom counted the money from the porch sale. "Did you make enough?" she asked hopefully.

"Almost as much as I'd hoped," Mom said. She put her arm around Lydia's shoulders. "Honey, God has a good plan for your future. He has it all worked out. You'll see. We just need to take it day by day as we watch his wonderful plan unfold."

"Mom, do you really believe that?" Lydia asked.

"Yes, I do. You know why? The Bible—God's Word to us—says so. He has a *good* plan for us. We can be filled with hope about our future."

Lydia didn't respond, but the future still seemed very uncertain to her. Her parents kept making decisions she had no control over. And now this move to a small apartment!

The day after the porch sale, Mom was up early. "I've found four apartments we can afford," she said. "I like different things about each one. Today, you girls will get to help me choose."

Lydia took a deep breath. If Mom believed God had a good plan for them, she would choose to believe it too. She chose to have hope for their future.

Several weeks later, after settling into their new home, Lydia decided some of the changes they'd had to make were good. She loved the swimming pool at her apartment complex. And the library was only two blocks away.

Going home to an apartment after school still didn't feel normal, but it was becoming the "new normal." Not only did Lydia choose to feel hopeful these days, she truly *felt* hopeful.

More to Explore: "O LORD my God, you have performed many wonders for us. Your plans for us are too numerous to list. If I tried to recite all your wonderful deeds, I would never come to the end of them." (Psalm 40:5 NLT)

Connecting to God: "Dear God, I feel so afraid of the future when things keep changing. Thank you for the wonderful plan you have for my life. Help me to trust you even more. Amen."

Journal Prompt: How can you change your negative thoughts?

Take Action: Sometimes, feelings are slow to change. You might have to wait awhile to see the answer to your prayers. What can you do in the meantime?

> *Situation:* You failed a math test.
> *Don't Say This:* "I'll *never* learn how to do this."
> *Say This:* "I know God will help me learn this if I'm patient."

> *Situation:* Your best friend moved away.
> *Don't Say This:* "I'm going to be lonely *forever*."
> *Say This:* "I trust God to bring me another good friend."

> *Situation:* You caught the flu and missed a fun party.
> *Don't Say This:* "This is so unfair! This *always* happens to me."
> *Say This:* "I'm disappointed, but there will be more parties this year."

Real-girl Confession: "Sometimes, I get scared about my future."

Indexed under: change, divorce

Devotion #46

"The one who is in you is greater than the one who is in the world."

(1 John 4:4)

"I Can't Change!"

Skylar had been having some very tough months. At the beginning of the year, she was an average-sized girl who laughed often. Then, things changed. Dad found a girlfriend and didn't want to be married anymore. Skylar stuffed down her sadness and anger, turning to food when she was upset. It worked for a while and helped her forget her troubles. But slowly, she gained weight. At first, she could hide it with looser clothes. Eventually, she was very overweight.

Skylar didn't like herself much anymore. She didn't like how she looked or that she couldn't bike without getting out of breath, and she had so little energy. *I'll change,* she thought one day. *I'll stop eating too much. I'll exercise and feel better!*

Even though she tried really hard, Skylar found she couldn't stop overeating for long. The food was too tempting. And there were still many times when she was upset about her family situation. She was even more upset that she couldn't change herself.

One day, she took a deep breath and confided in her friend's mom. "Mrs. Lewis, you lost a lot of weight last year, and now you play in tennis tournaments. How did you do it?"

"Are you wanting to lose some weight?" Mrs. Lewis asked.

"I've really tried, but as you can see, I haven't been successful. I can't do it!"

"No one can do it alone," Mrs. Lewis said. "But you're a believer—you've trusted Jesus as your Lord and Savior—so you have Jesus living inside of you. When you rely on Jesus, you can overcome anything."

"Really?" Skylar asked, feeling hope for the first time.

"Just remember that you can't do it alone. Philippians 4:13 says, 'I can do everything *through him* who gives me strength.' Pray and ask for God's help to overcome the temptation to eat too much. Food won't fix your feelings. Let God help you instead."

It took some time, but Skylar finally learned to turn to God when she was tempted to eat more than she needed. Slowly but surely, she returned to the girl she used to be—only stronger.

More to Explore: "The temptations in your life are no different from what others experience. And God is faithful. He will not allow the temptation to be more than you can stand. When you are tempted, he will show you a way out so that you can endure." (I Corinthians 10:13 NLT)

Connecting to God: "Dear God, so often I don't know how to deal with my feelings. Please help me and show me a healthy way to express myself so I don't turn to unhealthy habits. Amen."

Journal Prompt: Do you use food as fuel? Or do you use it to feel better when you're bored or lonely?

Take Action: Many people give up trying to lose weight because they feel deprived of their favorite foods. You don't have to give up your favorite foods. You are free to eat anything you like. Just limit yourself to three bites of your treat. Close your eyes and *slowly* enjoy each bite. Studies have shown that your taste buds are much less sensitive after three bites of anything. The first three bites are always the tastiest! So enjoy three bites of a treat from time to time. It will help you stay on your eating plan.

Real-girl Confession: "My mom called me chubby the other day, and I broke out in tears."

Indexed under: divorce, overweight, temptation

Devotion #47

"O Lord, you are so good, so ready to forgive, so full of unfailing love for all who ask for your help."

(Psalm 86:5 NLT)

Coming Clean

Lara was having a bad day. She'd overslept, and as she was leaving the house, she shoved her little brother out of her way. She felt frazzled, so on the way to school, she spent her lunch money on candy at the convenience store. She'd forgotten her science report was due today, and she wasn't finished working on it. So she told her teacher she accidentally left it at home. That night, during family prayers, Lara had nothing to say.

Later, Dad asked her why she'd been so quiet.

Lara shrugged. "I don't know. I just didn't feel like talking to God."

"Hmmm." Dad was silent for a moment. Then he said, "Sometimes, I feel distant from God. Often, it is because I am trying to ignore some wrong things I've done. Instead of coming clean with God, I try to do other things with my mistake."

Lara blinked in surprise. "You do? Like what?"

"I make excuses about why I did it, like saying I had to speed or I'd be late to work."

Lara nodded with understanding. She hadn't wanted to get a bad grade on her book report, so she'd lied.

Dad sat down beside Lara. "Sometimes I cover up the sin, like hiding a bill I forgot to pay on time."

Lara could understand that, remembering how she'd hidden the candy wrappers.

Dad patted Lara's hand. "Mostly I get busy with other things so I can forget about it."

"Me too," Lara said. She remembered shoving her brother, then catching up with her friend to talk about their favorite TV show.

"The Bible defines sin as 'missing God's mark,'" Dad said, "or missing God's goal for you. When you carry around sins without confessing them to God, it's like food you forget that's in the back of the fridge. It might be sitting there for weeks, but you don't even remember it's there until it starts to stink. Sin doesn't stay hidden forever either."

Lara frowned. "Some of my sins feel like 'big' sins, but some feel so small that I forget about them."

Dad smiled. "Here's one problem with that. The sins don't go away when we ignore them. And we still experience the consequences."

"You're right," Lara admitted. Her book report had *still* received a lower grade. And her stomach had hurt all day from the candy she ate in place of lunch.

Lara asked God for forgiveness for how she'd acted — and she felt so relieved. Owning mistakes is like taking a wonderful, warm bath in God's love. God's mercy, love and forgiveness clean the guilt from your conscience and put peace in your heart.

More to Explore: "You are a God of forgiveness, gracious and merciful, slow to become angry, and rich in unfailing love." (Nehemiah 9:17 NLT)

Connecting to God: "Dear God, I've done something wrong, and I want to confess it to you. Please forgive me — and help me not to do it again. Amen."

Journal Prompt: An old Scottish proverb says, "Confession is good for the soul." What does that mean to you?

Take Action: How does a believer confess her sins? For a blueprint refer to 1 John 1:9 ! These are the basic steps:

1. Admit the wrong you did to God, and be specific. It might be something you did on purpose, such as lying, or something you didn't do, like refusing to help someone.
2. Tell God you're sorry and don't want to do this again.
3. Ask God for his help to change. You are not alone and have his support.
4. Thank God for his mercy and forgiveness and cleansing.
5. If necessary, do what you can to fix a problem concerning someone else. For example, tell the truth or give them a hand.

Real-girl Confession: "What a day! I need a do-over!"

Indexed under: distant from God

Devotion #48

"The LORD detests double standards."

(Proverbs 20:23 NLT)

Living with Liars

Dakota squirmed in the pew, wishing desperately that she didn't have to sit up front. But her dad, the pastor, required it as proof of "family support."

Next to Dakota, her mom read her Bible, as the organist played the opening music. Dakota wished she had the guts to ask Mom how she could sit there, Sunday after Sunday, knowing Dad pretended to be something he wasn't.

Sometimes, it almost made Dakota sick to her stomach. People thought she and her mom were so lucky. "So blessed!" the older ladies said. Even Dakota's friends thought her dad was wonderful and funny and *soooo* understanding.

If only they saw him behind closed doors.

That morning's sermon was about the Pharisees. They pretended to be so holy and so concerned about the common people, while laying a ton of backbreaking rules on them. Jesus had called the Pharisees "whitewashed tombs which appear beautiful on the outside, but inside are full of dead men's bones"—in other words, total fakes.

Dakota stared at her father during the sermon, as she was required to do. But she'd perfected a trick of staring at his left ear lobe while tuning him out. Otherwise, if she paid attention, she knew the contempt she felt would show on her face.

It was a struggle to respect her dad, since what he presented to the public was the opposite of his behavior at home. Dakota had read in her Bible that "the Lord detests double standards"—being one way with certain people and totally different with others. Jesus himself had had plenty to say about church officials who appeared righteous in public and were different in private.

God knew Dad's heart, Dakota was sure, and he knew Dakota's heart too. God helped her behave in a respectful manner and honor her father, even if she saw things she hated.

That day, over Sunday dinner, her dad complained about attendance and about the low offering. He blamed Dakota's mom for the altar flowers not getting delivered on time and for her not being more outgoing to the wealthier members of the church. "I ask so little of you," he said, banging his fist on the table. "I'd think you could get such simple things right."

Anger built in Dakota over the false accusations and blame. *I'm going to record you and play it for your deacons,* she wanted to scream. *Let them hear how you talk to us!*

She knew her mom wouldn't thank her for sticking up for her though. Dakota had done it before, but it only made her dad worse. "You must be respectful," Mom had told her. "God will honor you for that. You can't change your father's behavior, and neither can I. We must let God deal with him while we keep our peace."

Dakota hugged her mom tightly that night. Dakota didn't like the situation, but God helped her live with it. And he helped her have joy even in the midst of it.

More to Explore: "Then he said to them, 'You like to appear righteous in public, but God knows your hearts.'" (Luke 16:15 NLT)

Connecting to God: "God, you know how angry I get when I see my parent behaving so loving in public and then being abusive in private. Help me not to become bitter. And help me to be the same person myself, in public and in private. Amen."

Journal Prompt: When you don't respect a parent's choices, is it difficult to be respectful, as God has commanded?

Take Action: Do you sometimes act like a fake? Here are some signs:

When you do something nice for someone, do you call attention to it?

Do you obey the rules, but your heart is filled with hatred for others?

Do you wear special clothing to draw attention to yourself?

Do you have rules for others to follow that you don't follow yourself?

Real-girl Confession: "He's such a fake. I want to puke!"

Indexed under: abuse/emotional/verbal, anger

Devotion #49

"A friend is always loyal, and a brother is born to help in time of need."

(Proverbs 17:17 NLT)

A Trusted Friend

Jasmine visited her dad every other weekend at his new apartment. Even though she really missed her dad, those weekends were hard. She worried about him a lot. He always seemed so lonely and depressed. They usually sat in his dark, bare-looking apartment and watched a lot of movies. Then one weekend, it was different.

"I want you to meet someone," Dad said.

Jasmine stiffened. Did Dad have a girlfriend *already*? "Who is it?" she asked warily.

"His name is Mack, and he has two daughters. He moved into the apartment across the courtyard last week, and we met at the pool." He smiled. "Turns out we work at the same company! Just in different departments. They also go to my church."

"That's cool." Jasmine grinned, not because this was such great news, but because she hadn't seen her dad relaxed and smiley like that for months. It felt good to see that he wasn't as lonely. He seemed lighter inside somehow.

"I thought we'd have Mack and his girls over for a cookout this weekend. They're a lot of fun — I think you'll like them."

That night, Jasmine met Dad's new friend and his daughters.

It felt awkward at first, but slowly she grew more comfortable. By the end of the weekend, Jasmine was eager to see them again.

When it was time to say good-bye to Dad, Jasmine slipped her hand through his arm. "I'm glad you have new friends," she said. "I like Mack and his kids."

"Good," Dad said, patting her hand where it rested on his arm. "Mack has been a good friend to me, that's for sure. I hope his girls will become your friends too." He paused. "Just remember, though, that Jesus is the *best* friend you will ever have."

"I will, Dad."

"I wish I could be with you every day," Dad added, "but Jesus *is* always with you. You can't have a better friend than that."

More to Explore: "Go in peace, for we have sworn friendship with each other in the name of the LORD." (1 Samuel 20:42 NIV)

Connecting to God: "Dear God, my family has changed in ways that we didn't want, and sometimes we're all lonely. Please, bring friendly people into my life and my parents' lives. Help us to be open to getting to know them. Amen."

Journal Prompt: What are some positive things you can do when feeling lonely?

Take Action: It can help to fill lonely hours with extra sports activities, friends, hobbies, adventure and entertainment, but it might not be the *most* helpful thing to do. Your sense of loneliness is an opportunity for you to draw close to your heavenly Father, asking him what to do about your loneliness. "Listen to my prayer, O LORD, and hear my cry for help!" (Psalm 102:1 GNT). Tell God what is on your heart. He will always be your best friend.

Real-girl Confession: "Worrying makes me feel lonely."

Indexed under: divorce, friendship

Devotion #50

"As the deer longs for streams of water, so I long for you, O God. I thirst for God, the living God."

(Psalms 42:1–2 NLT)

How's Your Appetite?

Allison was getting used to her parents' divorce. She tried not to think about it. But when she did, it upset her, so she'd play a game on the computer or watch a DVD to take her mind off it. She could forget about the divorce for a while, but it never lasted. She was still afraid of the future and angry at her dad for leaving.

"I wish you would read your Bible and pray more," her mom said. "I start each day that way. I wouldn't get very far without it."

Allison shrugged. "I know I should, but I just don't feel like it," she said. "You'll think I'm a bad Christian, but reading my Bible and praying doesn't sound good."

"No, that doesn't make you a bad Christian," Mom said, "but it isn't wise either." She headed for the kitchen. "Come with me."

Puzzled, Allison followed Mom to the kitchen and perched on one of the stools at the counter. Mom pulled raw broccoli and baby carrots from the fridge and put some on a plate. "Here," she said.

Allison wrinkled her nose. "I have to be really hungry to

want raw veggies," she said. "I already ate a *good* snack after school."

"Exactly my point," Mom said, munching on a carrot. "Since I didn't fill up on cookies and soda, I'm hungry, and this carrot tastes really good."

Allison tilted her head to one side. "You've lost me. What's your point?"

"Just this," Mom said. "Sometimes you're hungry and thirsty, and other times you're full. When you're very hungry, healthful foods — like vegetables — taste good! But when you've filled up after school on sweets, those same foods at suppertime don't appeal to you at all."

"I get that part," Allison said, "but what's that got to do with praying and Bible reading?"

"The same thing can happen in your soul and spirit. If you don't feel like reading your Bible or praying, it might be that you're already 'full.' You might not be hungry for God because you're stuffing yourself with movies, TV shows, video games, and calling friends."

"Are you saying that stuff is bad?" Allison protested. "I watch good movies and clean TV shows. And you like my friends!"

"Don't get me wrong," Mom assured her. "You make good entertainment choices, and I appreciate that. But it can cause problems when you put it before God in your life." She ate another carrot, and then put the rest back in the fridge. "You can create hunger for healthful foods by saving the sweets for dessert. In the same way, you can create a hunger and thirst for God by putting off other pleasures for later."

"Do you do that?" Allison asked.

"I try to every day. I postpone watching a movie or losing myself in a book until I've spent time reading my Bible. Instead of calling a friend when I'm upset, I pray first and tell God what's on my heart." She gave Allison a hug. "Just give it a try. That's all I ask."

Allison began spending ten minutes with God as soon as she woke up in the morning. She did it again for ten minutes right after school, before doing anything else. In a couple weeks, Allison noticed a huge difference in her feelings. By seeking God first, she had more peace, she was much less angry, and she was no longer afraid.

More to Explore: "A person who is full refuses honey, but even bitter food tastes sweet to the hungry." (Proverbs 27:7 NLT)

Connecting to God: "Dear God, I spend so much time trying to fix — or forget — my feelings. Forgive me for not coming to you first with my feelings and problems. Amen."

Journal Prompt: List ten things you can thank God for right now.

Take Action: Some things you can do during your quiet time with God:

Play your favorite praise and worship songs.

Memorize helpful scriptures.

Read from a favorite devotional book.

Use a "read through the Bible in a year" plan.

Pray while sitting or going for a walk.

Write in a gratitude journal.

Real-girl Confession: "I just want to forget my problems."

Indexed under: distant from God, divorce

Devotion #51

"For your Maker is your husband—the LORD Almighty is his name."

(Isaiah 54:5)

"But You're My Mom!"

Alexa was barely used to the divorce, and now Mom was being chased by guys! How was she supposed to deal with *that*?

After Alexa answered phone calls from two different men, her stomach was tied in knots. First, a guy from church invited Mom to a concert. Then a man from work asked Mom to attend some business dinner with him. *Business*, Alexa thought. *Oh, sure.* The calls and invitations left Alexa unsettled—and afraid. She didn't know why, but she felt hurt too.

Just then, the doorbell rang. Mr. Jenkins from across the street asked for Alexa's mom.

"Why?" Alexa demanded. She didn't care if she sounded rude. "What do you want?"

Mr. Jenkins stammered a moment, and then said, "I noticed your grass is getting tall. I thought your mother might want me to mow it."

"I can mow it. Thanks anyway." Alexa slammed the door and burst into tears.

"Honey, what's wrong?" Mom asked, hurrying into the room.

"I hate Mr. Jenkins!" Alexa said. "I'm sick of guys calling you!"

"But I haven't gone out with anyone," Mom said, clearly puzzled. "And Al Jenkins is a good friend."

Alexa sniffled. "If Dad can't live here, then I don't want some other man around."

"Oh." Mom pulled her over to the couch. "You don't need to worry about that for a long time." She put a finger under Alexa's chin and tilted her head up. "I don't want a boyfriend. Not yet anyway."

"Really?"

"Really. God is my husband now. The Bible says so, and also that he's your Father. He provides for us and protects us. He's with us in every change we go through." She sighed. "But being new to the area, I *do* wish I had a girl friend. I'd like someone my age to talk to and do things with."

Alexa and her mother discussed it some more, brainstorming ideas for making friends in their new neighborhood. The following weekend, they volunteered to work at a nearby garage sale as a way to meet some neighbors. Mom made a couple girl friends, and Alexa was relieved when *they* were the ones who called and came over.

More to Explore: "I will make you my wife forever, showing you . . . unfailing love and compassion. I will be faithful to you and make you mine, and you will finally know me as the LORD." (Hosea 2:19 – 20 NLT)

Connecting to God: "Dear Lord, I feel scared and sad when there are big changes in our family. Please give me peace during these uncertain times. Amen."

Journal Prompt: How can prayer help you be calm during times of change?

Take Action: Are you lonely? Try one of these ideas:

Learn and practice a new skill, such as yo-yo, knitting, or juggling, and then show (and maybe teach) it to others.

Start a collection or a craft-making hobby. You will not feel as lonely, and you can talk about it with other people who are into the same things.

Write letters to pen pals. Many kids' magazines have a pen-pals page for kids wanting to make friends from around the world.

Real-girl Confession: "No one in the whole world understands how I feel."

Indexed under: divorce, friendship

Devotion #52

"These trials will show you that your faith is genuine. It is being tested as fire tests and purifies gold—though your faith is far more precious than mere gold."

(1 Peter 1:7 NLT)

Danger: Shifting Sand

Dawn sat at the kitchen table on Saturday morning during Christmas vacation, working on a sketch of a castle she intended to paint for a social studies project. Bent over the encyclopedia photo of a real castle in England, she measured and tried to accurately reproduce the proportions.

Mr. Engles would be so impressed with her part of the group project. She studied the way the drawbridge was built, then used her ruler to carefully sketch it into the front of the castle.

Dawn heard her mom get up and come out to the kitchen. Suddenly, without warning, Mom slapped Dawn on the side of her head. Her ear stung. Dawn swung around, her ear ringing.

"Don't you ignore me when I'm talking to you!" Mom yelled.

"I wasn't!" Dawn protested.

Mom grabbed the ruler off the table and hit Dawn three times. "When I talk to you, you listen to me!"

"Stop!" Dawn cried. "I really didn't hear you." She rubbed the back of her head. "I was working on my drawing for social studies."

Mom got her mug of coffee and the newspaper, and then went back to her room. With relief, Dawn heard the bedroom door slam.

After Dawn finished her sketch, she spent the day in her bedroom, to stay out of the line of fire. She sat in her chair and looked out the window, still upset from her mom's attack. She honestly hadn't been ignoring her. Dawn hadn't heard her say anything. Mom erupted with no warning—and it wasn't the first time. Dawn just wished she had a way to predict her mom's behavior.

She opened her Bible and read, knowing it would bring her comfort and peace after a while. And it did, when she came to Hebrews 13:8. "Jesus Christ is the same yesterday, today, and forever," Dawn read aloud. She sighed and smiled. Knowing Jesus would always be the same and never change would help her with Mom's unpredictable behavior. It reminded her of the Sunday school song about building her house upon a rock, so that when the storms came, the house would still stay standing. Jesus was that Rock.

Late in the afternoon, Dawn came out of her room to get a snack. Mom was stretched out on the couch, watching a movie. "Did you finish your homework?" she asked.

Dawn nodded. "Yes," she said, wondering how her mom could act like nothing had happened that morning. No apology. Nothing.

Dawn brought her snack to the living room and watched the rest of the movie. All seemed peaceful, but Dawn knew it was only temporary.

Her mom could be a different person by tomorrow—or even an hour from now. There was no way to guess. But Jesus would be the same, Dawn reminded herself. Since she had built her house on the Rock, with the Holy Spirit's help, she could withstand any storm.

More to Explore: "All of creation will be shaken and removed, so that only unshakable things will remain." (Hebrews 12:27 NLT)

Connecting to God: "Dear God, when I look at some people in my life, I get afraid of what they might do. Please help me remember that you are always the same, and you can overcome anything. Help me stay focused on you. Amen."

Journal Prompt: How do you feel about a recent event or situation in your life?

Take Action: Things to do when someone is angry:

1. Stay calm; reacting with more anger can only make it worse.
2. Let the angry person vent, but stand back out of the way. Show you are listening.
3. Talk to a trusted adult (pastor, school counselor, teacher, a friend's parent) if physical abuse is happening. In that case, you and your parent both need help.

Real-girl Confession: "Whenever my mom gets angry, she turns into a psycho!"

Indexed under: abuse/physical

Devotion #53

"Can anything ever separate us from Christ's love? Does it mean he no longer loves us if we have trouble or calamity, or are persecuted, or hungry, or destitute, or in danger? No, despite all these things, overwhelming victory is ours through Christ, who loved us."

(Romans 8:35, 37 NLT)

"You Dumb Klutz!"

Nicole sang to herself as she dried dishes after supper. Suddenly one of Dad's coffee cups slipped from her fingers, hit the tile floor, and shattered.

"What broke?" Dad yelled from the living room where the TV blared.

"A cup," Nicole called. "Sorry."

"You dumb klutz!" he shouted, storming into the kitchen. "Can't you even do something simple like the dishes? What do you use for brains?"

Nicole froze in place. *Stop it, Dad!* she cried silently. She fought back tears as she swept up the broken pieces, telling herself he didn't mean it. Even so, if her own dad thought she was a stupid klutz, she decided she probably was.

While Dad got more snacks from the refrigerator, he reminded Nicole of all the mistakes she'd made lately. "You're hopeless," he said before going back to watch TV.

As Nicole finished the dishes, she felt sadder and sadder. *Am I really so terrible?* Nicole asked herself. Why didn't her dad love her the way other dads in the neighborhood loved their kids? Did anyone love her? It sure didn't feel like it.

In her bedroom later, she reached for her library book, and her bookmark fell out. The bookmark had been a Christmas gift from her Sunday school teacher. On the front was a Bible verse telling how God loved her so much that he'd sent his Son to set an example and show the way to heaven. On the back of the bookmark, the teacher had written, "To Nicole, one of my brightest stars!"

Nicole closed her eyes and smiled. Yes, there *was* someone who loved her. She sang softly, "Jesus loves me, this I know, for the Bible tells me so ..."

More to Explore: "I am convinced that nothing can ever separate us from God's love. Neither death nor life, neither angels nor demons, neither our fears for today nor our worries about tomorrow ... can separate us from God's love." (Romans 8:38 NLT)

Connecting to God: "Dear God, sometimes it seems like nobody loves me. Help me remember that you always love me, no matter what, now and forever. Amen."

Journal Prompt: Write down ways you can ignore hurtful people and love yourself like God loves you.

Take Action: God never lies, and below are things he says about you. Read often!

For you were made in my image. (Genesis 1:27)

I chose you when I planned creation. (Ephesians 1:11 – 12)

You are fearfully and wonderfully made. (Psalm 139:14)

It is my desire to lavish my love on you. (1 John 3:1)

I offer you more than your earthly father ever could. (Matthew 7:11)

I am the perfect father. (Matthew 5:48)

I am your provider, and I meet all your needs. (Matthew 6:31–33)

My plan for your future is filled with hope. (Jeremiah 29:11)

I love you with an everlasting love. (Jeremiah 31:3)

Real-girl Confession: "I always wanted to make Dad proud, but that's never gonna happen."

Indexed under: abuse/emotional/verbal

Devotion #54

*"When I was a child, I talked like a child, I thought like a child,
I reasoned like a child. When I became a man, I put the ways of
childhood behind me."*

(1 Corinthians 13:11)

Taking the Blame

Tiffany and her younger sister never talked about the divorce,
even to each other. Tiffany talked about everything else, but
not that. Why? Because Tiffany knew the divorce was her
fault.

If only I'd kept our room cleaner, Tiffany thought, *and not
picked on Sophie.* Tiffany remembered all the times Dad had
asked her to be more patient with Sophie. She also remembered
Dad yelling at her to clean up her room, and how she'd argued
with him.

One day, Tiffany went to her closet for a clean shirt and
found Sophie huddled in a corner crying. Tiffany knelt beside
her on the floor. "Sophie, what's the matter?"

"I miss Daddy!"

"Me too," Tiffany said.

"But it's my fault he went away!" Sophie wailed.

"*Your* fault? No, it's not!"

"Is so!" Sophie sniffled and rubbed at her eyes. "Remember
all those times I wouldn't go to bed on time? I kept asking for a
drink of water, and I spilled it, and Daddy had to clean it up."

"You think *that's* why he left?" Tiffany asked. "I acted worse than you. It was *my* fault he left, not yours."

Just then, Mom peeked into the closet. "I had no idea either of you felt this way." She sat down beside them. "What adults do is *never* a child's fault. Children behave in certain ways, like picking on each other or having trouble going to bed, but those actions never make adults choose to do wrong things. Adults make decisions on their own."

Tiffany wished she could believe her mom's words. "How do you know that?"

"The Bible teaches in many places that we are each responsible for our own actions," Mom said. "Some people call it being *accountable* for your actions."

Tiffany glanced at her sister, then Mom. "It's really *not* our fault Dad left?"

"Not even one tiny bit. Dad still loves you so much. His leaving had nothing to do with you." Mom pulled them close. "Just keep being the wonderful girls you are. Life will get better in time. You'll see."

More to Explore: "You judge me by human standards, but I do not judge anyone." (John 8:15 NLT)

Connecting to God: "Dear God, I'm afraid that I'm to blame for what's going wrong in my family. Help me to remember that I'm only responsible for *my* actions, not my parents' decisions. Amen."

Journal Prompt: Does your mind go around and around like a hamster on a wheel when you're upset? How can you stop that?

Take Action:

"I can't control other people's behavior."

"I am responsible for *my* actions — not yours!"

"I can't make someone change."

Real-girl Confession: "I must have made a mistake so bad that my dad went away."

Indexed under: divorce, thoughts

Devotion #55

*" 'My thoughts are nothing like your thoughts,' says the LORD.
'And my ways are far beyond anything you could imagine.' "*

(Isaiah 55:8 NLT)

"I Don't Understand!"

Maddy didn't understand why it had to be *her* dad who lost his job in the cutbacks at the factory. Then, her parents got a divorce instead of working things out. Maddy had prayed for a miracle, and she *really* didn't understand why Dad left. After that, Grandpa died from a heart attack. *Why?* Maddy wanted to scream. Why were bad things happening to her?

She knew that she wasn't the only one who had to deal with bad things. The nightly newscast was full of disasters. Maddy didn't understand why God hadn't changed the path of the hurricane so it wouldn't destroy whole towns. She didn't understand tsunamis or school shootings or parents who abused their kids.

Some nights, after watching TV programs and news shows, she couldn't fall asleep. When she did, she sometimes had nightmares. One night, after dreaming she was covered in hot lava while trying to escape an erupting volcano, she sat up screaming.

"Honey! Wake up!" Her mom shook her gently. "You're having a bad dream."

Maddy shivered and opened her eyes. "Thank heavens! My legs were burning from hot lava!"

"Well, it was only a dream," Mom said, rubbing her back. "It won't happen to you since there isn't a volcano within five hundred miles."

Maddy smiled, but then her smile faded. "That's true, but plenty of other bad stuff has happened to us lately. I don't understand why."

Mom sighed. "Often we don't understand why bad things happen. God is in total control of this world, and nothing happens without his permission. Believe me, when I'm having a hard time, I also ask, 'God, why is this happening?'"

"Does God tell you?"

"Sometimes, but not always and usually not for a long time. But we can be sure of one thing: Nothing happens by accident or chance."

"Even stuff like volcanoes and earthquakes?" Maddy asked. "Or Grandpa dying?"

"Yes, even that is under God's control. God has a good reason for even our most painful experiences."

"That's hard to believe," Maddy muttered.

"That's because we don't get to see ahead of time how the Lord will use bad times for our good. Usually, we find out after some time passes, as long as we keep trusting God through our tough times and our pain."

"I just wish I understood *now* why bad stuff happens."

"Well, God's ways won't always make sense to you. The Bible, in Isaiah 55:9, teaches that his ways and thoughts are higher than ours. And remember, God sees the whole picture—he knows what the future holds."

Maddy's future did settle down in time. Within a month, Maddy's dad found a better job. Her parents forgave each other and became friends. Maddy's pain over losing her grandpa grew less and less, until finally she only remembered the happy times. Peace settled over Maddy's life once again.

More to Explore: "Just as the heavens are higher than the earth, so my ways are higher than your ways and my thoughts higher than your thoughts." (Isaiah 55:9 NLT)

Connecting to God: "Dear God, I don't understand why my family has to go through this hard time. Help me to trust you that you have a good plan for our lives and to be patient while I wait to see the good. Amen."

Journal Prompt: How does watching the news or reading the newspaper affect you?

Take Action: Give yourself some "disaster relief."

TV shows, newspapers, and magazines increase ratings and sales by focusing on disasters. They talk in great detail about natural disasters (floods, tornadoes, blizzards, earthquakes, shark and alligator attacks) and man-made disasters (shootings, bombings, wars, abuse). *Turn it off and turn away from it.* You don't need to know all the details or know about every bad thing that happens. Instead, focus on stories in the news about the good things people do, the heroes, the generous people, and the funny stories. God is doing miracles every day in people's lives, but our world doesn't report much of it. So actively hunt for it. Focus more on the good things in the world, and you'll feel better (Philippians 4:8).

Real-girl Confession: "Some nights, I'm afraid to even close my eyes."

Indexed under: crisis, thoughts

Devotion #56

"This hope is a strong and trustworthy anchor for our souls."

(Hebrews 6:19 NLT)

Smashed Hopes

After many tests, doctors discovered Samantha's older brother had bi-polar disorder. With treatment, Jon's mood swings evened out over the summer. He rarely embarrassed Samantha anymore by arguing in public, laughing wildly in a theater, or having fistfights with the neighbors.

Samantha was eager for the new school year to begin. "People in normal families don't know how lucky they are," Samantha told her best friend. "Now I'm not afraid to go home. I might even try having a friend over." With Jon doing better, she could join after-school clubs and sports activities instead of hurrying home to help protect her younger sister.

All of Samantha's hopes came crashing down the first week of school. Jon refused to continue treatment. Without his medicine and counseling, he reverted to yelling and throwing things and staying up all night playing video games. The fear of violence kept Samantha tense every evening.

Samantha was bitterly disappointed! She'd had such hopes for this year. Now her life was like a stormy sea again. Huge waves threatened to fill her boat—and sink it. When Samantha described her life to her Sunday school teacher, he told her how

Jesus could be her anchor. "An anchor holds a boat in place, whether the sea is calm or it's stormy with rough waves."

"But I want a calm life, not a stormy one!" Samantha cried.

"I know, but what you *need* is for your mind and feelings to be calm, no matter what. If you let him, Jesus will be your anchor and keep your boat steady, regardless of how much Jon stirs up the water."

Samantha sighed. "But I was going to join an acrobatics club at school and sing in choir. Now I can't."

"There's no reason to cancel your plans," her teacher said. "You can—and should—still live your life."

Samantha felt a surge of hope. Yes, she *would* do that. And she would let Jesus keep her calm when Jon stirred things up at home. She could *still* have a fun school year.

More to Explore: "Yes, my soul, find rest in God; my hope comes from him." (Psalm 62:5)

Connecting to God: "Dear God, when my family is having problems, I feel like they are *my* problems too. Help me to trust you to keep me anchored and stable while I live the life you gave me. Amen."

Journal Prompt: How can you have a normal life when a family member keeps things stirred up all the time?

Take Action: Truths to remember about mental illness:

No one is to blame for the illness.

Mental disorders affect more than the person who is ill.

You have a right to ensure your personal safety.

Your role is to be a sibling or child, not a parent or caseworker.

It is important to have boundaries and to set clear limits.

Real-girl Confession: "I don't want to make things worse for my parents, but I hurt too."

Indexed under: disappointment, health/health crisis

Devotion #57

"Forgive us our sins, for we also forgive everyone who sins against us."

(Luke 11:4)

Unwise Words

Melanie hurried home after band practice, excited about being chosen to march with the high-school band at Friday's out-of-town football game. Her stepdad, Jeff, loved football, so Melanie knew he'd drive her to Morristown.

She dropped her clarinet, music, and backpack on the kitchen counter. "Hi, Mom. Is Jeff home?"

"He's in the garage fixing the mower," Mom said.

Melanie found her stepdad in the garage with the lawn mower in pieces. "Hey, Jeff, want to go to a football game?"

"Hey there, Mel." Her stepdad waved a greasy hand at her. "I'd love to go. When?"

"Friday night. I need a ride to Morristown to play in the halftime program."

He frowned and wiped his hands on a greasy rag. "This Friday?"

"Yep. We have to leave the minute you get off work."

Her stepdad slowly shook his head. "I'm sorry, but Sarah needs me to drive her to her mom's Friday night. Her car—"

"I should have known!" Melanie snapped. "You keep saying you're *my* dad now too, but obviously it's your *real* daughter who's important!" She stomped back into the house and ran up to her room.

Sitting by the window that overlooked the backyard, she watched Jeff close the garage door, his shoulders slumped. She turned her back on the window, and her gaze fell on the framed plaque by her desk. It was First Corinthians 13, the "love chapter." She read the words about love being patient and love being kind and love not keeping a record of wrongs. Melanie bit her lower lip. She never should have talked to Jeff that way. Jeff had shown over and over this past year that he cared about her.

God, I'm sorry. He doesn't deserve what I just said to him, Melanie thought.

She hurried down to the kitchen where Mom was cooking supper. Jeff and Sarah were putting together a salad. "Jeff," Melanie said, clearing her throat, "I'm sorry about what I said. Would you forgive me?"

Jeff turned and gave her a bear hug. "You bet, hon," he said. "No problem."

After supper, the family worked out a plan to get Melanie to her football game.

More to Explore: "If we claim we have no sin, we are only fooling ourselves and not living in the truth." (1 John 1:8 NLT)

Connecting to God: "Dear God, sometimes I do or say things that hurt others. Please forgive me for this, and help the person I've hurt to forgive me too. Amen."

Journal Prompt: What kind and healthy ways can you use to release pent-up emotions?

Take Action: When people are upset, they do things to feel better. Some things help, but others can make them feel worse. Which is which?

watch TV (help? yes/no) (make it worse? yes/no)

eat junk food (help? yes/no) (make it worse? yes/no)

pray (help? yes/no) (make it worse? yes/no)

cry (help? yes/no) (make it worse? yes/no)

call friends (help? yes/no) (make it worse? yes/no)

yell at someone (help? yes/no) (make it worse? yes/no)

go for a run (help? yes/no) (make it worse? yes/no)

Real-girl Confession: "I have to compete for attention in my step-family."

Indexed under: stepfamilies

Devotion #58

"He who keeps you will not slumber. The LORD is your keeper. The LORD shall preserve you from all evil; He shall preserve your soul."

(Psalm 121: 3, 5, 7 NKJV)

Alone in the Night

Abby woke in the middle of the night and reached sleepily for the glass of water on her nightstand. As she raised it to her lips, she suddenly remembered that her mom was in the hospital. Mom's appendix had burst, and even after the emergency surgery, Mom was terribly sick. Dad was staying with her at the hospital. Abby wasn't allowed to see Mom or even talk to her on the phone.

Down the hall, Grandma was sleeping in the guest room. Abby wasn't really alone, but she *felt* alone.

She lay in bed, wide awake, even though her glow-in-the-dark clock said it was 3:15 a.m. She stared at the ceiling, wondering if Mom was awake at the hospital too. Abby wished she could see her.

A *thunk* somewhere in the house made Abby jump. *Someone's breaking in!* she thought. *And Grandma's too old to save me!* Then she realized that the *thunk* was just the refrigerator's ice maker dumping some ice. Even so, there were lots of other creepy creaks and bumping noises in the dark house.

Pulling the blanket up to her nose, Abby recalled Grandma's words at bedtime. "If you're ever afraid in the night," she'd said, "remember that it's the Lord who keeps you — and he never sleeps. God needs no sleep. He is always listening for your cries."

"How do you know that, Grandma?" Abby had asked.

"Well, the Bible calls the Lord your *keeper* — he will *keep* and protect your soul. It's like when I stay with you."

Abby smiled. "That's why Mom says, 'Grandma will *keep* the kids'?"

"Exactly! When parents have to leave their children, they choose someone they trust to put in charge. God is always our trusted keeper, and he cares for us better than any earthly mom or dad — or grandma — ever could."

Dwelling on that comforting thought, Abby snuggled down in her covers, whispered her prayers, and fell asleep.

More to Explore: "You are my hiding place; you will protect me from trouble and surround me with songs of deliverance." (Psalm 32:7)

Connecting to God: "Dear God, my problems seem bigger in the dark, and I'm scared that things won't turn out okay. But I trust *you* to take care of me and watch over me. Amen."

Journal Prompt: What does the following quote mean to you? "Courage does not mean that you are not afraid. Doing something that you are not afraid of is easy. Doing or facing something that you *are* afraid of takes courage."

Take Action: Ways to avoid being frightened at night:

When lying in bed, exercise your creative muscles. Make up a happy story in your mind — you be the main character.

Write down each worry that is troubling you on a slip of paper; pray, and give it to God, then tear up the paper.

Play a CD you like, or set a playlist on "repeat all" to help you sleep.

Use a cool night-light or lava lamp to chase away the shadows.

A pet cat to cuddle or a big dog lying on your feet is a comfort!

Real-girl Confession: "Sometimes, the nights are so very long."

Indexed under: fear, health/health crisis

Devotion #59

"You were running a good race. Who cut in on you to keep you from obeying the truth?"

(Galatians 5:7 TNIV)

Following the (Wrong) Leader

Alya looked from one hand to the other. She couldn't believe it! Usually she had nowhere to go on the weekends. Now she had to choose between two invitations for the same day!

One birthday invitation was from Lila, a girl at church she'd known since kindergarten. Lila's party would be at her house. Alya guessed it would include birthday cake, some fun games, and maybe a video.

The other invitation was from Tia, a girl at school whose birthday was also Saturday. Tia's party was being held at the new Kid Carnival, a huge entertainment mall that included a theater, a pizza place, a Mexican diner, a kids' shooting range, carnival rides, and more! Tia was pretty bossy and sometimes talked rough, but her party sounded like a lot more fun.

Alya threw the first invitation in her wastebasket. Then she went to ask Mom's permission to go to the second one.

Alya had a fabulous time at Tia's party. She loved the rides, even though she ate too many candy bars and tamales. The movie Tia chose was PG–13, which Alya knew she wasn't allowed to see, but everyone else walked right in. Alya didn't have the nerve to say anything and hurried in with the group.

Tia's parents were there, so how bad could it be? Alya just wouldn't mention it to Mom.

After that weekend, Alya was included more often in Tia's after-school and weekend plans. One Sunday, Tia invited Alya to go to the lake and swim all day. When Alya asked, Mom said, "You know the answer is no if you have to miss church to go."

"That's not fair!" Alya cried, stomping her foot.

"Ex*cuse* me?" Mom said, one eyebrow raised.

"Why can't I go just this once? It's special."

"You can go to the lake after church, but you're not skipping church to go."

Alya exploded and threw down her phone. "I hate you!"

Mom took several deep breaths. "Go to your room. I'll be in to discuss this in half an hour." She picked up the phone and handed it to Alya. "Don't forget to call Tia to let her know you can't come."

Later in Alya's bedroom, Mom sat down beside her on the bed. "We need to talk about some disturbing changes I've seen in you lately."

Alya hung her head. "I know I blew up. I'm sorry."

"I forgive you," Mom said. "But I'm concerned about your quick temper, the mouthy back talk, the defiance of rules. It's not like you."

Alya shrugged. "I don't know why," she said. She honestly didn't know why she'd turned into a smart mouth. "Maybe it's hormones?"

Mom smiled. "Some of it might be," she agreed.

Alya glanced sideways at her mom. "But that's no excuse, is it?" She sighed. "I'm sorry about the bad temper and back talk."

"You're forgiven," Mom said. "Some of these changes may be growing pains, but I suspect that part of it is the company you've been keeping. For a long time, you've been doing a great job, 'running a good race,' as the Bible says. But something—or someone—cut in on you and is getting you off course."

Alya looked up. "You mean Tia?"

"Well, I know your behavior started going downhill when your friendships changed."

Alya nodded. She knew Mom was right, and actually it was a relief to talk about it. Some of the things Tia had wanted to do lately really bothered Alya. She knew they were wrong.

"I *do* miss my old friends," Alya admitted. "If I'm not grounded, how about if we invite Lila to come to the lake with us this weekend—*after* church?"

More to Explore: "Who has bewitched you that you should not obey the truth?" (Galatians 3:1 NKJV)

Connecting to God: "God, lots of times I already know the right thing to do, but I'm afraid to take a stand. Give me courage to do the right thing, even if it means losing a friend. Amen."

Journal Prompt: Who is the hardest person to say no to? Why?

Take Action: Resisting pressure is hard sometimes. Why?

You might…

be afraid of being rejected

want to be liked

not want to lose a friend

not want to be made fun of

not want to hurt someone's feelings

not know how to get out of the situation

What to do?

> Pray for help and strength.
>
> Stand up straight.
>
> Look the person in the eye.
>
> Say no like you mean it.

Real-girl Confession: "I didn't want to look like a baby."

Indexed under: anger, peer pressure

Devotion #60

"Love each other with genuine affection."

(Romans 12:10 NLT)

Hidden Love

Kelsey didn't talk about it, but the divorce had left her feeling unloved and unwanted. It was especially hard on the weekends she visited Dad. He rarely talked to her beyond, "How was your week?" He turned on the TV while they ate. In the car, the radio was too loud to talk over. The worst part was at night. At home, Mom tucked her in with lots of hugs. Kelsey didn't want to be a baby, but she loved the hugs. Dad almost never touched her.

One night, he stopped in her bedroom doorway, said goodnight, and reached for the light switch. "Dad, wait!" Kelsey said. Then, to her horror, she burst into tears.

Dad stepped into her bedroom. "Kelsey? Honey?" He came closer. "What's wrong?"

Kelsey felt foolish, but she couldn't hide her feelings anymore. She missed her dad's affection. *Lord, please help me say this without hurting Dad's feelings.*

She took a shaky breath. "Why don't you love me anymore?" she whispered.

Dad's face turned red. He moved to stand by her bed and awkwardly patted her shoulder. "I *do* love you," he said. "I miss you all the time."

Kelsey wiped her tears with the back of her hand. "Then why don't you ever hug me? Or hold my hand? Or talk to me about things?"

"I'm sorry," Dad said, handing her a box of tissues. "I don't know why. Maybe because my parents never hugged me, at least not that I remember." He shrugged. "Your mom was always the hugger in the family."

"She still is," Kelsey said. She paused, then took a deep breath. "But I need the dad kind of hugs too."

Dad smiled and held out his arms, and Kelsey wrapped her arms around his neck. Dad patted her back for a long time.

The next day at the zoo, Dad held Kelsey's hand two different times. When they ate ice cream, they sat under a shade tree while Kelsey told Dad about her friends. She was so glad she'd spoken up about her real feelings. This was going to be the best weekend she'd had all year with Dad.

More to Explore: "All of you should be of one mind. Sympathize with each other. Be tenderhearted, and keep a humble attitude." (1 Peter 3:8 NLT)

Connecting to God: "Dear God, sometimes it feels like no one loves me. I'm glad you love me, but I need people to show it too. Help me to pay attention to others the way I want them to love me. Amen."

Journal Prompt: "Whoever is happy will make others happy, too." (Mark Twain) How can you think more about *giving* attention to others than *getting* attention?

Take Action: We all like to receive attention. Some things we do to get attention are positive. But some things are negative and hurtful to ourselves or others. Which is which?

1. Clean the kitchen without being asked. (positive/negative)
2. Dress in clothing that is too revealing. (positive/negative)
3. Become the class clown to entertain your friends. (positive/negative)
4. Win a ribbon at the science fair. (positive/negative)
5. Play "fetch" with your dog at the park. (positive/negative)
6. Talk back to your parents when asked to do something. (positive/negative)

Real-girl Confession: "Sometimes, I feel totally invisible, like nobody sees me at all."

Indexed under: divorce, honesty

Devotion #61

"The LORD is good to those who depend on him, to those who search for him. So it is good to wait quietly for salvation from the LORD."

(Lamentations 3:25–26 NLT)

Running Ahead of God

Gracie didn't enjoy babysitting, but she was grateful for the money she made watching two children next door during the summer. The best part of the job was playing with the Johnsons' two golden Labs. The babysitting money was okay, but it wouldn't be enough to replace her stolen bike. "God, I need to earn more money," Gracie prayed. "I'll need a bike next month when school starts!"

The very next day, Mrs. Johnson had a surprise for Gracie. "We'd like you to come with us next week to a conference we're attending. You'll babysit during the day. Then we'll take over at night, and you'll be free to do what you want. The conference center even has a pool and a game room." The pay would be enough for Gracie to buy a bike.

Gracie had an uneasy feeling about accepting the job, but she agreed to go anyway. She didn't see how else God could answer her prayer. It was a challenging week, but Gracie got through it and was paid.

A week after the conference, Gracie discovered that while

she was gone, Mr. Wall had called from the animal shelter where she volunteered.

Gracie dialed the shelter number. "Mr. Wall? I got your message."

"I called because I needed an assistant to help with the animals."

"I'd *love* that job!" Gracie cried.

"I'm sorry." Mr. Wall paused. "When you didn't call back, I hired a young man instead."

"Oh." Gracie swallowed hard. "I understand." Gracie hung up, wishing with all her heart that she'd listened to her doubts and waited on God. He'd had the perfect job waiting for her!

If you sense in your heart that God is saying "no" or "wait," remember that he knows much more than you know. God may be saving you from a big disappointment. Or he could be preparing a great blessing for you to enjoy. Pray, and don't be in a big hurry. Wait for God's perfect timing.

More to Explore: "I wait for the LORD, my whole being waits, and in his word I put my hope." (Psalm 130:5 NIV)

Connecting to God: "Dear God, I don't know what to do. I need you to show me the right steps to take. Help me to not run ahead of you, but wait patiently for your answer. Amen."

Journal Prompt: If you knew the answer to your prayer would arrive one week from today, what would you do differently this week?

Take Action: Reasons why God may require us to wait for our answer include...

What we want is right for us, but we are not yet ready for it.

God wants to teach us discipline through waiting.

Getting what we want right now would hurt someone else.

God wants to teach us to depend on him, not ourselves or others.

Real-girl Confession: "I just want to take control!"

Indexed under: finances, needs, waiting on God

Devotion #62

"My God will meet all your needs according to the riches of his glory in Christ Jesus."

(Philippians 4:19)

"What Do I Really Need?"

Jordan was staring out the window when her Sunday school teacher grabbed her attention. "Do you need a friend?" he asked. "Do you need a pair of shoes? Or good advice? Whatever you need, God promises to provide for his children's needs."

Jordan sat up straight. She needed all those things!

"God is the one who supplies everything you need," the teacher continued. "He gives your parents jobs so they can provide you with clothing and food. He gives wisdom in the Bible and through other godly people. He *will* provide everything you need."

Jordan shrugged. "God has more important things to worry about than what I need."

"No, if the need is important to you, it's important to God too," her teacher said. "Nothing is too small to take to God — or too big for him to supply."

At home, Jordan asked Mom if she believed God would provide everything they needed.

"I sure do," Mom said. "But I don't always *know* what I need."

Jordan frowned. "That doesn't make sense."

"Well, I might think I need to relax in front of the TV, but I *really* need to take a walk or a bike ride. You might think you need to study for two hours, when you *really* need to study one hour and then get some sleep." She winked at Jordan. "I've learned to ask God what I really need—and then ask him to supply it."

That night Jordan decided to pray a new way. "God, I'm tired and sad. I think I need a friend who could give me some good advice," she said. "And I'd love a new pair of shoes, but right now we don't have money for them." She snuggled down under her quilt. "I don't honestly know what I really need, God, but you know. Please give me what I need."

Then Jordan went to sleep peacefully, eager to see how God would supply her needs.

More to Explore: "For the LORD God is our sun and our shield. The LORD will withhold no good thing from those who do what is right." (Psalm 84:11 NLT)

Connecting to God: "Dear God, thank you for meeting all my needs, no matter how big or small. Help me to recognize the difference between my true needs and my wants. Amen."

Journal Prompt: Why is it sometimes hard to believe that God will meet your needs?

Take Action: Some ways God provides for your needs include...

    Giving you a gift or donation from someone

    Giving you a good idea to solve the problem

    Showing you how to make your money go farther

    Providing you with a job to earn the necessary money

Giving you strength to go to work

ALL of the above are God's provision!

Real-girl Confession: "I wish I had more money smarts!"

Indexed under: finances, needs

Devotion #63

"My health may fail, and my spirit may grow weak, but God remains the strength of my heart; he is mine forever."

(Psalm 73:26 NLT)

When Disaster Strikes

Juliana was disappointed—terribly disappointed. Her older brother had been wounded a year ago while serving overseas in the army. She'd been waiting all that time for him to come home. Juliana's parents had been able to visit him in the hospital in Texas, but children weren't allowed. Jason had endured three operations to save his torn-up leg. But a month ago, the doctors said the leg had to come off. It wasn't healing well at all.

Jason was finally coming home today—but with only one leg. *What should I say?* Juliana wondered. *What should I do?* She used to run up and jump on his back, or he'd swing her around in a big circle. He couldn't do those things anymore—or play tag with her or go bowling. He'd be in a wheelchair until he was fitted with his artificial leg. Would he feel like her big brother anymore?

In a few hours her parents would be home with her brother. Juliana knelt by the couch and told God about her fears and frustration. "God, why did this have to happen? I don't know what to do!" she prayed. "Show me how to be the kind of sister he needs now." As she waited quietly, ideas started coming to Juliana. She could share favorite books with her brother. She could teach him how to play chess. They could watch funny movies together. He'd still be her big brother — just in new ways.

At first it was awkward, but Juliana learned to relate to her brother in new ways. One day as they played catch in the backyard, Juliana asked him, "How do you do it?"

"Do what?" Jason asked, making a funny face at her.

"Stay happy with just one leg," Juliana said, coming to stand by his wheelchair.

"Some days are harder than others," Jason admitted. He paused. "All people go through tough times, kiddo. What you do then makes all the difference. Hard times can destroy people — I've seen it happen. But hard times can also help you walk closer with God. That's what I choose ... every day."

Juliana hugged Jason's neck. She had never been so proud of her big brother.

More to Explore: "Though the fig tree does not bud and there are no grapes on the vines, though the olive crop fails and the fields produce no food ... yet I will rejoice in the LORD, I will be joyful in God my Savior." (Habakkuk 3:17 – 18)

Connecting to God: "Dear Lord, my situation looks like a disaster to me. I don't see any way out. But you know the reasons for this, and I trust you. Show me the right things to do now. Amen."

Journal Prompt: What would I do if a family member were wounded and disabled?

Take Action: How can you help?

Alone, or with your family and friends, or as a class project, you can raise money for wounded warrior funds.

Send Thanksgiving, Christmas, and Easter cards to wounded warriors who are hospitalized.

When you see soldiers, shake their hands and thank them for serving their country.

Reai-girl Confession: "He will never be the same again. Never."

Indexed under: crisis, health/health crisis

Devotion #64

"He will yet fill your mouth with laughter and your lips with shouts of joy."

(Job 8:21)

It's Okay to Laugh

Kia twirled her straw in her chocolate milk as she told Mom about her day at summer school. She'd loved everything but the swim class. "The teacher made us blow bubbles like little babies," Kia said.

Mom laughed. "It isn't just babies who blow bubbles." She thought for a second. "Fish blow bubbles." She grinned. "Even moms blow bubbles."

Mom leaned over her glass of milk and blew through her straw. Chocolate bubbles filled her glass and popped. Kia couldn't believe Mom was breaking her own strict rule about not blowing bubbles at the table!

Grinning, Kia grabbed her own straw and blew. Before long, popped milk bubbles had splattered the table. Then, just as suddenly, Kia stopped. Something was wrong. She blinked, stared at Mom, and then left the table and headed to her bedroom.

Mom followed her and stood in her bedroom doorway. "What's wrong?" she asked. "Do you feel sick?"

"No, not really." Kia twisted her fingers together in her lap. "It's just that ..."

Mom waited. "Just what, honey?"

Kia took several deep breaths. "We were sitting there ... laughing ... having fun." *And it makes me feel guilty*, she added silently.

Mom frowned and tilted her head to one side. "Is that a problem?"

"It's not right somehow." Kia shrugged. "You're getting a divorce. I'll bet Daddy's not laughing right now."

"I don't know if he is or not," Mom admitted, sitting down beside Kia on the bed, "but it's okay to laugh and have fun anyway." She smiled. "The Bible says laughter makes a person healthier and that a 'merry heart' works like medicine. Laughter can be especially healing when you're going through tough times."

"Then why does it feel wrong?"

"I don't know. Sometimes we feel guilty for feeling happy if someone we love is unhappy. But God doesn't want that. He knows that a cheerful heart is good, like medicine."

Mom gave Kia a giant hug, and then tickled her ribs. Kia rolled back on the bed and burst into laughter.

More to Explore: "A merry heart does good, like medicine." (Proverbs 17:22 NKJV)

Connecting to God: "Dear God, sometimes I just want to forget my problems for a while and laugh. Please help me to have fun without feeling guilty. Thank you for the gift of laughter! Amen."

Journal Prompt: If you feel sad, do you want your friends to give you sympathy or tell you jokes to cheer you up?

Take Action: Health benefits of humor include...

Laughter relaxes the whole body. A good, hearty laugh relieves stress.

Laughter boosts the immune system. Laughter improves your resistance to disease.

Laughter triggers the release of endorphins, the body's natural pain reliever.

Laughter protects the heart. Laughter improves the function of blood vessels and increases blood flow.

So create opportunities to laugh!

Watch a funny movie or TV show.

Share a good joke or funny story.

Check out your bookstore's humor section.

Do something silly.

Make time for fun activities, such as bowling, miniature golf, or roller skating.

Real-girl Confession: "I almost forgot how to laugh this year."

Indexed under: divorce, guilt

Devotion #65

"I say, love your enemies! Pray for those who persecute you!"

(Matthew 5:44 NLT)

Doing Good — to Enemies?

Lyndsey was afraid all the time. She was especially afraid when her cousin Jason babysat. She was worried before he came over, and she had nightmares after he left. Everyone else liked Jason, but Lyndsey didn't.

He stole her birthday money and threatened to smack her if she told. When he was mad at someone else, he yelled at Lyndsey or hit her. He made her watch movies she hated. She cried, but it just made Jason laugh. Lyndsey hated Jason. She wanted to tell someone, but she wondered if anyone would believe her. Jason was always friendly to grown-ups, but he could be so mean to Lyndsey when no one else was looking.

One night, Lyndsey's mom caught a glimpse of Lyndsey's bare back and the swollen marks Jason had made when he hit her. Crying and shaking, Lyndsey finally told Mom the whole story.

Mom reported everything to the police, and they took action so Jason couldn't hurt Lyndsey again. Lyndsey was glad, but shocked when Mom later said they should also pray for Jason.

"Why?" Lyndsey asked. "Jason never even said he's sorry!"

"Jason needs God," Mom said. "As believers, we need to forgive him and do good things for him."

Lyndsey drew back. "No! I don't want him around again!"

"He won't be," Mom assured her. "Forgiving and loving an enemy doesn't mean he can still do bad things to you. We can't allow abuse to continue. Reporting Jason to the police was doing a *good* thing for him. It stopped him from sinning and will give him a chance to change."

Lyndsey nodded slowly. "I could pray for him," she said.

"I'll write to him at the boys' home where he lives now," Mom added.

Lyndsey was glad to know she could pray for Jason, but she didn't have to be around him. She could stop being afraid. It felt so good to be safe again!

More to Explore: "If your enemy is hungry, give him bread to eat; and if he is thirsty, give him water to drink." (Proverbs 25:21 NKJV)

Connecting to God: "Dear God, I want this person to stop hurting me! Protect me, show me what to do, and give me the courage to tell someone what is happening. Amen."

Journal Prompt: Were you ever afraid to tell someone that another person hurt you? (It is never too late to tell someone you trust!)

Take Action: Do you suspect a friend is being physically abused? Here are some signs:

Frequent injuries or unexplained bruises, welts, or cuts

Injuries appear to have a pattern, such as marks from a hand or belt

Flinches at sudden movements

Seems afraid to go home

Wears odd clothing, such as long-sleeved shirts on hot days, to cover up injuries

Real-girl Confession: "I'm in a box with no one to tell."

Indexed under: abuse/physical, fear, worry

Devotion #66

"Jesus Christ is the same yesterday and today and forever."

(Hebrews 13:8 NASB)

Can't Things Stay the Same?

Rachel stood at the curb, waiting until Adriana's moving van was out of sight. Fighting back tears, she ran into the house. "I hate this! This is my third best friend to move away!"

Rachel didn't think she could stand losing another friend. At the beginning of the school year, one of her friends went to live with her grandmother because her mother was very sick. At Christmastime, another good friend moved when her father was deployed in the army. And now her next-door neighbor, her very best friend for three years, had to move after her dad found another job far away.

"I'm sorry, sweetheart," Mom said. "I know Adriana hated to move too. But they had to go where her dad could find work."

"I know," Rachel said. "It's nobody's fault, but I'm still going to be lonely. Why can't things ever stay the same?"

Her mom hugged her close. "I'm afraid that isn't the way life works. We need to learn how to survive the changes—and let God help us come out even stronger."

Rachel slowly nodded. Then she prayed silently, *God, I don't know how to handle this change. Please show me how.*

"I know Adriana will have more adjustments than I will," Rachel admitted. "A new home, a new school, a new church, new kids everywhere ..."

"Yes," Mom agreed. "Some situations bring a lot of difficult changes, like the death of a relative or a parent losing a job. Most changes are less serious—like having friends move away."

"It's still hard!" Rachel said, fighting back tears.

"I know. You and Adriana can keep in touch by phone or email or Skype calls, as often as you want. Your love for each other won't change because of the distance."

Rachel nodded slowly. "I'll do that, but I still wish she wouldn't move."

"I know. Some years, you'll experience big changes like this; other years, you'll experience smaller changes you barely notice." Mom tilted her head to one side and studied Rachel. "And *you* are always growing and changing too. So is everyone else in our family."

Rachel sighed. It sounded overwhelming! "How am I supposed to handle all these changes?"

"Remember the Bible verse about Jesus being the same yesterday, today and forever?" Mom asked. "That's how we handle life. Instead of focusing on the changes we don't want, we focus on Jesus who is the unmoving Rock. He's like an anchor that keeps our boat stable when the waves get high."

Hmmm, Rachel thought, *Jesus never changed?* Then that meant he *always* loved her, *always* protected her, was *always* with her, and *always* wanted her to talk to him. She smiled at that comforting thought. No matter what else changed in her life, Jesus stayed the same! She could count on it.

More to Explore: "You are the same, and Your years will have no end." (Psalm 102:27 NKJV)

Connecting to God: "Dear Lord, I don't like when things change. I want life to stay the same, but I know that isn't going to happen. Help me to adjust to the changes. Thank you that I can always count on you to be the same. Amen."

Journal Prompt: Things keep changing! How can you handle the uncertainty in your life?

Take Action: Unexpected changes are harder because we did not know they were coming and were not ready. Which changes below are "expected," and which are "unexpected" changes?

You have a substitute teacher for the day. (expected/unexpected)

December is so cold you need gloves and a scarf. (expected/unexpected)

You are given a pop quiz. (expected/unexpected)

You woke up with a temperature. (expected/unexpected)

Your baby brother is born. (expected/unexpected)

Real-girl Confession: "I wanted things to change, but not this much!"

Indexed under: change, loneliness

Devotion #67

"Those who wait on the LORD shall renew their strength; they shall mount up with wings like eagles, they shall run and not be weary, they shall walk and not faint."

(Isaiah 40:31 NKJV)

Torn Between Two Choices

Mariah was being asked to make the hardest decision of her whole life. Not only were her parents getting a divorce, but she had to go to court and choose which parent to live with.

I can't do that, Lord, she prayed. *It's not right that I have to choose!*

The pressure was strong from both sides.

"I'll be terribly lonely if you choose to live with Dad," Mom said.

"If you live with me," Dad said, "you'll get your own room and a big allowance. I want you to have the child-support money, but your mother just spends it."

"I have no choice about the money," Mom said. "Food and rent cost so much!"

Mariah was confused and didn't know what to do. She had to make a decision very soon, but there were no *good* choices. She didn't want to hurt either parent. That night, she knelt by her bed and prayed a long time, asking God which parent to choose. After an hour, she still sensed no answer except, "Wait!"

So that's what Mariah did. Neither choice felt right, so she waited. When her parents asked for her decision, she said she didn't know yet. Finally, the pressure was too much, and Mariah confided in her best friend's mother.

"You're doing the right thing, Mariah," Mrs. Baker said. "If the time isn't right, or your way is not clear, then *wait* on God. It's not time to make the decision yet."

"But it's really hard!" Mariah said. "Mom and Dad keep asking me about it."

"I'm sure it's incredibly difficult," Mrs. Baker agreed. "But hang in there. Even if you feel pushed by others, *wait*. If you feel a sense of urgency in your own spirit, but the choice feels wrong, then *wait*. If God hasn't made the way clear, do not plunge forward. *Wait!*"

Tears that Mariah had been holding back for days welled up and spilled over. "Why is waiting such a good idea?" she asked.

"Well, if you've prayed about a hard decision," Mrs. Baker assured her, "you can trust that God is working things out—maybe in you, or in someone else, or in your circumstances. It takes time to get things in place. Waiting is wiser than making a hurried decision."

Mariah continued to wait and pray, and wait some more. It wasn't easy. The answer came, finally. Mariah's parents decided to share her time equally—so Mariah never had to choose. She was glad she hadn't allowed herself to be pressured into making such an important decision. She was so grateful that God worked out the decision for her.

More to Explore: "Wait on the Lord; be of good courage, and He shall strengthen your heart; wait, I say, on the Lord!" (Psalm 27:14 NKJV)

Connecting to God: "Dear God, I don't know what to do, and I'm afraid of making a wrong decision. Please guide me and give me patience to wait until you make the answer clear. Amen."

Journal Prompt: Are you waiting for something right now? How do you feel while you wait?

Take Action: What is God doing while you wait?

Helping you grow in patience and trust

Working in the hearts of other people in order to answer your prayer

Preparing you for the answer he has in mind

Protecting you from unseen danger that he knows is down the road, but you don't

Helping you understand that your hope must be in God alone — not in your own abilities

Real-girl Confession: "I can't wait any longer!"

Indexed under: divorce, waiting on God

Devotion #68

"You will go on your way in safety, and your foot will not stumble. When you lie down, you will not be afraid; when you lie down, your sleep will be sweet."

(Proverbs 3:23–24)

"Please Stop Fighting!"

Shaking in fear, Nikki pulled the covers over her head, but she could still hear the yelling. Her older sister was in trouble again, and Dad's shouting matched her sister's screaming. Every weekend was the same thing. Her sister stayed out too late with her boyfriend. When she got home in the middle of the night, she and Dad would fight, and Nikki would be jerked out of a sound sleep.

If they only fought with words, Nikki thought she could ignore them. But more than once, Dad had hit her sister. *Please shut your mouth!* Nikki silently begged her sister. *Don't keep pushing him!* But the shouting grew worse, louder and louder. If only it weren't so late. Otherwise, Nikki could sneak next door to Mrs. Hood's house where she felt safe. The older neighbor understood Nikki's fears.

Then, Nikki remembered something Mrs. Hood had recently read to her out of her Bible. It was about praying for help and about how God would take care of things for her. "You can safely give the scary situation to God," Mrs. Hood had said.

"Really?" Nikki asked her neighbor. "Have you ever been this scared?"

Mrs. Hood smiled. "Oh my, yes. But in those scary times, I learned that the Lord is my helper. Friends and neighbors can offer some help—and I'm glad to do it—but God is the only one powerful enough to really protect you and bring peace in your family." She took Nikki's hands in her own. "Let's pray together right now for God to make your home safe and that he will give you some much-needed rest."

Nikki put her head under her pillow to block out the fighting and prayed like Mrs. Hood had prayed that day. She poured out her worries to God. She asked for protection for her sister and healing for her family. Then she thanked God for watching over them.

After some time, Nikki felt a sense of peace cover her like a soft blanket. And before long, she went to sleep.

More to Explore: "I lift up my eyes to the mountains — where does my help come from? My help comes from the LORD, the Maker of heaven and earth." (Psalm 121:1–2)

Connecting to God: "Dear Lord, sometimes I am so afraid for my family — and myself! Please help me feel your presence, and give me peace and a safe place. Amen."

Journal Prompt: What do you think the following proverb from India means? "Anger is as a stone cast into a wasp's nest."

Take Action: Three common parent-kid fights to avoid — discuss calmly instead!

1. The "It's Not Fair" Fight ["Other kids get to stay out late, but I have a curfew!"]

2. The "Treat Me Like A Grown-Up" Fight ["I am old enough for a cell phone with unlimited texting."]

3. The "We Are a Different Person" Fight ["I want you to join the band," Dad says. "But I want to play volleyball," the pre-teen says.]

Real-girl Confession: "I'm so sick of the fights I could scream!"

Indexed under: fear, worry

Devotion #69

"A gentle answer turns away wrath, but a harsh word stirs up anger."

(Proverbs 15:1)

Dodging Land Mines

Shelby felt like she spent her life tiptoeing around hidden land mines. "I'm always trying to avoid some kind of explosion," she complained to her best friend, Katie. "At school, Erin is constantly picking at me and trying to start a fight."

"She's just jealous of you," Katie said. "She wishes she were as smart and pretty as you."

Shelby shrugged. "Then at home, there's Dad. Ever since he lost his job, he's been like a bear woken from hibernation." She frowned. "I don't remember the last time he just talked to me without growling. No matter how hard I try, or how I explain things, everything ends up in a fight."

Katie nodded. "When my big brother gets like that and tries to pick a fight because he's mad, I'm polite and use really short answers. It usually stops him."

"Really?" Shelby asked. "How'd you think of doing that?"

"I didn't," Katie said. "But I've got a cool Sunday school teacher who talked to me about it once. She overheard my brother picking on me in the parking lot, and she told me later that the Bible had a lot of practical advice about dealing with angry people."

"It does?" Shelby asked. That was a surprise to her.

"Yes, it says that a soft answer turns away wrath." At Shelby's puzzled expression, she added, "It means that a gentle answer can sooth anger, or make anger disappear."

Shelby thought about Katie's advice the rest of the walk home. She was putting away her lunch bag when Dad came out to the kitchen. "Where have you been?" he snapped.

Shelby jumped and glanced at the clock. She wasn't late. "I just walked home from school."

"School got out half an hour ago! It doesn't take that long to walk home!"

Shelby's heart pounded. "I had to go to my locker, and then—"

"Don't lie to me!" Dad thundered. "What have you really been doing?"

Shelby's knees shook, and she took a deep breath. *Lord, help me to be calm*, she prayed. Then she remembered Katie's advice: Be polite and give short, soft answers.

"I helped the band teacher put away music," Shelby said. "Then I walked home."

"Next time you're going to be late, call first!"

But I'm not late, Shelby wanted to argue. *Stop being mean to me!* Yet she knew that defending herself would just keep the fight going. "All right," she said softly. "I will."

Dad waited, but Shelby said no more. Finally he left, and Shelby sighed with relief. *Thank you, Lord!*

More to Explore: "Let your conversation be gracious and attractive so that you will have the right response for everyone." (Colossians 4:6 NLT)

Connecting to God: "Dear God, I feel attacked when grouchy people try to pick fights with me. Show me how to give honest and gentle answers so I don't keep arguments going. Show me how to have peace. Amen."

Journal Prompt: How do you handle it when someone falsely accuses you of something?

Take Action: Sometimes, we can accidentally trigger someone's anger with our words or actions. Avoid the following in conversation with an angry person:

> Saying, "So?"
>
> Turning your back when they are speaking
>
> Saying, "Whatever ..."
>
> Interrupting
>
> Walking away
>
> Saying, "Calm down!"

Real-girl Confession: "I'm afraid he'll go from yelling to hitting."

Indexed under: anger

Devotion #70

"Make allowance for each other's faults, and forgive anyone who offends you. Remember, the Lord forgave you, so you must forgive others."

(Colossians 3:13 NLT)

Payback!

Autumn slammed her bedroom door. "I've had it! Jackson's going to pay for this!"

She threw herself down on her bed, but she was too mad to cry. Why couldn't Mom keep Jackson out of her stuff? First he tore her jacket, then colored in her books, and now this! She'd had her scooter only two weeks! After school, she'd come home to find the back part broken off.

"He's just curious. He didn't mean to break anything," Mom said as Autumn stormed off.

Scowling, Autumn rolled over and sat up. That little brother of hers needed to be taught a lesson. Ever since Dad left, Jackson had been "accidentally" breaking things. Well, no more. "Wait until he sees how it feels," Autumn muttered. "I'll break his Transformer!"

She slipped across the hallway to Jackson's bedroom, grabbed the Transformer he'd received for his birthday, and carried it back to her room. Sitting with the toy on her lap, Autumn tried—but couldn't make herself break it. Then the tears came.

She knew it was wrong to pay her brother back, but it was so unfair of him to damage her stuff.

"Lord, I know I'm supposed to forgive him. I need you to help me do it, because I sure don't want to!" Autumn prayed. After a few minutes, Autumn was determined to do what God commanded, and she gave up her idea of revenge. She carried Jackson's Transformer back to his room.

Then Autumn went to talk to Mom. "I need your help to protect my things when I'm at school. I'm not angry with Jackson, but it's not fair what he does."

"You're right," Mom said. "Forgiving Jackson about the scooter doesn't mean he's allowed to continue breaking things. We need to remove temptation from him for a while."

Autumn let out a sigh of relief that Mom understood. "Can I lock my scooter in the shed? And can I get a lock put on my closet door?"

"I don't see why not," Mom said. Together, Autumn and Mom worked out ways to keep Jackson away from her things.

More to Explore: "When you stand praying, if you hold anything against anyone, forgive them, so that your Father in heaven may forgive you your sins." (Mark 11:25)

Connecting to God: "Dear Lord, sometimes I get so mad about things people say or do to me. I ask you to help me forgive them and give up any ideas of payback. And thank you for forgiving *my* sins too! Amen."

Journal Prompt: When you're upset, how can you calm down so you don't do something out of revenge?

Take Action: Avoid fights with younger siblings, but protect your stuff in these easy ways...

Kitchen cabinets out of a small child's reach can be used to store small items that are valuable to you.

Waterproof storage boxes are an ideal place to keep items out of sight and out of reach. They can be hidden under your bed or on a top shelf.

Filing cabinets that lock are an excellent place to store items you want to protect and keep safe, like small toys, drawings, letters, and money.

Real-girl Confession: "I could just scream! It's not fair."

Indexed under: anger, revenge

Devotion #71

"Every time you criticize someone, you condemn yourself. It takes one to know one. Judgmental criticism of others is a well-known way of escaping detection in your own crimes."

(Romans 2:1 MSG)

Sticks and Stones

McKenna was the tallest person in her class. And the skinniest. She wasn't sure, but she thought she also had the biggest feet. She was always tripping over them, making kids laugh.

She absolutely *hated* gym class. Everyone expected her to be good at basketball and volleyball, just because she was tall. She wasn't athletic, though. She was awkward and clumsy. She pretended to think it was funny when classmates called her Bean Pole, Stick, and Klutz.

But it wasn't funny. The name-calling hurt.

McKenna tried to be invisible. She never raised her hand in class, she never volunteered for anything, and she dressed in browns and blacks. During class, she slouched down in her seat, hoping to disappear.

"Stop slouching and sit up tall," her teacher said. "Do you want to develop a curved spine?"

"Be proud of your height!" Mom said. "You might be a basketball player or a model someday."

For months, McKenna ignored the name-calling or smiled as if it were a joke. She tried asking them to please stop, but no one listened. It was wearing her down. Who did these kids think they were, anyway? None of them were all that gorgeous. It would feel so good to yell back, "Yeah, I'm skinny, but it's better than being a tub of lard like you!" But she didn't.

Then one Sunday, her pastor talked about how God had a plan for each person, and that he had already prepared work for each person to do. God had also created each person differently so they'd be able to do the work he had planned.

"God didn't use a cookie cutter when he made people," the pastor said. "Each of you is special and made the way you are for a special reason. Your purpose is unique, and your physical qualities and mental gifts will help you fulfill your purpose."

McKenna stared at her long legs and large feet, seeing them in a new light. Had God made her taller than others for some special reason?

"You might not know your purpose for many years, but God has known from the beginning," the pastor said. "So don't compare yourselves to others. No one is better or more valuable than anyone else. God loves us equally. We are his dearly loved children."

That afternoon McKenna went for a quiet walk and talked to God. She told him how she felt about the name-calling, and she asked him to refresh her worn-out spirit. She also asked him to show her the truth—how God saw her. That night in her Bible, McKenna found many promises from God about his everlasting love, his protection, and his willingness to meet her needs. She especially loved one verse that said, "So let's not get tired of doing what is good. At just the right time we will reap a harvest of blessing if we don't give up" (Galatians 6:9 NLT).

More to Explore: "This means that anyone who belongs to Christ has become a new person. The old life is gone; a new life has begun!" (2 Corinthians 5:17 NLT)

Connecting to God: "Dear God, please change how I feel about people's unkind words. Help me to remember every day that I am your precious daughter, and that that's all that really matters. Comfort me and remind me how much you love me just the way I am. Amen."

Journal Prompt: Why do people's words — even when they're lies — hurt so much?

Take Action:

Things to remember when facing or healing from verbal attacks:

"I'm a daughter of the King, the creator of the whole universe!"

"I'm the apple of God's eye, and my name is tattooed on the palm of his hand."

"I'm wonderfully made, a real masterpiece!"

"God has a good plan for my life."

"I am clothed in strength and dignity."

"God, my Father, always loves me."

"I walk in confidence."

Real-girl Confession: "If only I could turn invisible!"

Indexed under: abuse/emotional/verbal, criticism, thoughts

Devotion #72

"Treat others the same way you want them to treat you."

(Luke 6:31 NASB)

Ho-Ho-Ho ... Not!

Mia helped her mom carry down boxes of Christmas decorations from the attic. Although Christmas was her favorite holiday, this year she almost wanted to skip it. It was their first Christmas as a blended family.

"Now to set up the artificial tree," Mom said. "Then we'll be ready to decorate after supper."

Mia had been an only child for ten years, and now she had an older stepsister. Taylor was a pain, always bossing her around. When Mia heard Taylor's car in the driveway, she gritted her teeth.

Taylor slammed the front door and stared at the bare tree in the window. "What's that ugly thing?" she asked.

Mia fumed. "It's our Christmas tree, and it's not decorated yet." *You dork*, she wanted to add. Instead, she said, "We have boxes of decorations to put on it." She took a deep breath, remembering what Mom had said: *Treat your stepsister how you want to be treated yourself.* "You're welcome to help decorate."

Taylor snorted as she pawed through the decorations. "What a lot of junk," she said. "Half of this stuff looks homemade."

Mia glared at her through narrowed eyes. How *dare* she say that!

Taylor headed upstairs, but paused and added, "I'll set up our little silver tree tonight on that table in the corner. We have glass ornaments and porcelain figurines—very classy."

Mia stormed out to the kitchen where Mom was rolling out biscuit dough. "Taylor said our tree was junky!" she snapped. "They've got some dinky little tree that goes on a table! Don't they even know how to do a Christmas tree?"

Mom continued to roll out the dough. "It doesn't sound like either of you girls is being very open-minded," she said, "or very kind."

"What?" Mia demanded. "Taylor's the one being nasty!"

"Look, honey," Mom said, cutting the dough into biscuits, "you need to do what the Bible says and treat Taylor the way *you* want to be treated." She slid the cookie sheet of biscuits into the oven. "We decorate one way, and they decorate a different way. Neither one is *wrong*." She set the timer. "No matter what Taylor says, treat her the way you'd like to be treated, okay?"

Mia raised one eyebrow, but finally nodded. She didn't want to spoil the evening.

Several hours later, after both trees were decorated, Mia smiled at Taylor. "Yours is different," she said, "but it's very pretty too." And surprisingly, Mia found she really meant it.

More to Explore: "Love your neighbor as yourself." (Matthew 22:39 NLT)

Connecting to God: "Dear God, when people are mean to me, I want to be mean right back. Help me to forgive them instead and treat them the way I want to be treated. Amen."

Journal Prompt: How you *think* about people determines how you *feel* about them. Could you think differently about your stepsibling?

Take Action: Which thoughts will help you feel better about your stepsibling?

> *She's so mean!* OR *I wonder if she's upset about something.*
>
> *What a social misfit!* OR *Maybe she'd like to borrow my jacket.*
>
> *She's such a fake!* OR *I wonder why she's pretending to be happy.*
>
> *What a crybaby!* OR *I bet she's missing her mom.*
>
> *What a show off!* OR *She must be used to getting lots of attention.*
>
> *I can't stand her!* OR *Little by little, we can learn to be sisters.*

Real-girl Confession: "I used to hate her, but now she's my best friend."

Indexed under: revenge, step-families

Devotion #73

"Then Jesus said to his disciples, 'If any of you wants to be my follower, you must turn from your selfish ways, take up your cross, and follow me.'"

(Matthew 16:24–25 NLT)

"I Have Needs Too!"

Lucy's home was a happy one, and she was the oldest of six children. She spent her time at home changing diapers, bouncing crying babies, washing dishes, and folding clothes. She did her homework after the youngest children were in bed at night. Mom was grateful for her help, and Lucy felt needed and important. And *tired*. She learned not to ask for anything for herself because Mom was always too tired or too busy.

One Sunday she yawned repeatedly in Sunday school class. Her teacher, Miss Sharod, jokingly asked if she'd been up all night.

Lucy smiled. "It feels like it," she said. "The two sisters I share a room with both have bad coughs. They needed drinks of water every hour or so all night long."

"A big family sounds like a lot of work," Miss Sharod said. "I'm sure your parents appreciate your help."

Lucy started to say more, but then she saw the envious look on her friend Sara's face. Sara was an only child and had plenty of time to herself, but Lucy wouldn't have traded places.

Sara was home alone—a lot. Her mom worked nights, and

her dad spent evenings at the tavern. Lucy knew that by the time Sara was five, she had learned to make her own meals and put herself to bed. Lucy had visited Sara's home a couple of times, and she felt invisible there. It was like Sara's parents had forgotten their daughter even existed.

The lesson that morning was from Matthew 16. Lucy was familiar with the verses where Jesus taught his disciples to not be selfish, but instead take up their cross and follow him. Lucy fought to stay awake during class. *At least I don't have to feel guilty about being selfish*, she thought sleepily. She never had time to do anything fun for herself.

Lucy's mind wandered, but suddenly, Miss Sharod said something that startled her. "Some kids grow up believing what they want or need isn't important," the teacher said. "They've learned that taking care of themselves is selfish, including getting enough rest and having some fun."

"But isn't that what Jesus taught?" Lucy blurted out.

"No," the teacher said. "Jesus *did* teach that we are to put aside selfish desires, but he did *not* mean neglecting yourself. For example, if you refused to help your sister with her homework so you could watch TV all day, that's selfish. However, taking some time for yourself is *not* selfish. Everyone needs some rest and fun to be healthy. It's as important as food and air."

Lucy was embarrassed at the tears that welled up. Could that be true? Did God really want her to have some fun sometimes and not always be working?

"You might be required to do more work than other kids," Miss Sharod added. "That can happen for many reasons. But God knows you need rest and recreation too. Most important, you need time alone with God, who promises to meet all your needs. He will give you the strength you need for all that you have to do."

Lucy smiled then. If that was true, the first thing she planned to do that afternoon was take a nap!

More to Explore: "The Lord said to her, 'My dear Martha, you are worried and upset over all these details! There is only one thing worth being concerned about.'" (Luke 10:41–42 NLT)

Connecting to God: "Dear God, people seem to forget that I have needs too. You promise to meet all my needs, and I trust you to do that for me. Thank you! Amen."

Journal Prompt: Do you think your needs are important to God? Why or why not?

Take Action: Examples of taking care of yourself . . .

staying home when you're sick

valuing and taking quiet time alone and with God

taking time to read a book or sit outside or watch a movie

admitting you need some help and turning to a parent, teacher, or counselor

saying "no" to doing someone's homework or chores for them

taking a nap

Real-girl Confession: "What I need never seems important to anyone."

Indexed under: needs, overloaded

Devotion #74

"My enemies lay traps. Those who wish me harm make plans to ruin me. All day long they plan their treachery. I choose to hear nothing, and I make no reply."

(Psalm 38:12, 14 NLT)

Laying Traps

Mikayla looked forward to her mother's wedding because on that day, Mikayla would gain both a father and a sister. Her new stepsister, Piper, was the same age, so Mikayla expected they would be best friends in no time.

It turned out just the opposite. Piper was rude, but Mikayla tried to be understanding. It must be hard, she reasoned, moving into someone else's house. Mikayla ignored Piper's behavior, but then worse things happened. Piper lied, saying Mikayla copied Piper's homework. Then she accused Mikayla of sneaking out at night when she was supposed to be doing her homework. Mikayla couldn't prove it, but she'd been in her room the whole evening.

Mikayla's mom didn't believe Piper, but Piper's father did. "Are you calling my daughter a liar?" he demanded.

Mikayla's mom shouted back, "Are you calling my daughter a sneak and a cheat?"

Mikayla couldn't understand why Piper did those things to her. It had stirred up so much trouble between them and between their parents. Why? Mikayla prayed that the truth would come out. As she lay on her bed, she found comfort in a psalm. "I am waiting for you, O Lord. You must answer for me, O Lord my God" (Psalm 38:15 NLT). She went to sleep that night, trusting that God would provide a solution to her problem.

One evening, after their parents went to a meeting, Mikayla found Piper in the laundry room. She felt an inward nudge to bring up the problem. "I want to talk to you," Mikayla began.

"Get out of my way!" Piper said, starting to push past her.

"Please, wait." Mikayla's voice was gentle and kind. "Piper, why are you doing this? I like *you*. I was really looking forward to being friends."

Unexpectedly, tears welled up in Piper's eyes. "I want my real parents back together," she finally said, wiping her eyes. "For that to happen, I need to break up *this* marriage."

Mikayla took a deep breath and prayed for the right words to say. "So you lied about me to make Mom and Dad fight and break up?" Mikayla slowly shook her head. "I'm sorry you're unhappy here, but they won't let you make that decision for them."

"I know ..." Piper's voice trailed off, and she stared at the floor.

"Hey!" Mikayla grinned suddenly and poked Piper's arm. "Since you're going to be around, we might as well be friends. What do you say?"

More to Explore: "You love evil more than good and lies more than truth. You love to destroy others with your words, you liar!" (Psalm 52:3 – 4 NLT)

Connecting to God: "Dear God, I hate when people stir up trouble and don't want to get along. Please heal whatever is wrong, and give us peace. Amen."

Journal Prompt: When does being falsely blamed for something hurt your feelings? When does a false accusation make you angry?

Take Action: When falsely blamed for something, try not to (1) attack back, or (2) defend yourself. Here are some things you can say that are true and can end the attack:

"I guess we don't remember that incident the same."

"We will have to agree to disagree about that."

"I'm sorry you see it that way."

"I think I'm right, but I could be wrong."

Real-girl Confession: "Her accusation was a punch in the stomach."

Indexed under: stepfamilies, waiting on God

Devotion #75

"Trust in the LORD with all your heart and lean not on your own understanding; in all your ways submit to him, and he will make your paths straight."

(Proverbs 3:5–6 NIV)

"I'll Make You Pay!"

Fiona stopped in the convenience store after school for a candy bar. When she came around the corner of the aisle, she spotted her big brother, Logan, and two of his friends. Her heart sank when Logan dropped several cigarette lighters in his pocket.

Fiona turned to leave, but her brother ran up and grabbed her arm. "If you say anything," Logan said, "I'll make you pay." He pinched her arm hard, and Fiona bit her lip to keep from crying out.

Leaving the store without buying anything, Fiona hurried home. What should she do? Her stomach churned as she thought of first one idea, and then another. If she told Dad that Logan was stealing, he and Logan would have another big fight. Afterward, she knew Logan would also "make her pay" in some painful way. But if she kept quiet, Fiona feared things would only get worse. Last week, she'd overheard Logan and his friends joking about stealing a car.

At home, Fiona went directly to her room. She was scared and confused, wondering which way to turn. Then, her gaze fell on the book on her nightstand: her Bible. She held it and prayed, then read different passages of God's promises, like, "In my distress I called to the LORD; he answered me and set me free. The LORD is with me, I will not be afraid; what can anyone do to me?" (Psalm 118:5–6 GNT). Finally, calmness settled over Fiona's heart. Within half an hour, she knew what she had to do. She went to tell her mom.

More to Explore: "Don't be impressed with your own wisdom. Instead, fear the LORD and turn away from evil." (Proverbs 3:7 NLT)

Connecting to God: "Dear Lord, when I'm scared I don't know what to do. Please calm my heart and mind so that I can clearly hear from you about what to do. Thank you for helping me. Amen."

Journal Prompt: How can you trust God with a scary situation?

Take Action: Before the invention of the compass, sailors found direction by studying the stars. But what happened when it was overcast or foggy? They couldn't see the stars and had nothing to steer by. They became lost in the fog, or their ships crashed into hidden rocks. The Bible is your compass for "steering" your *life*. If you refuse to use your compass, your life can crash too, or you can lose your way. **Reading your Bible** and **praying** is like using that compass. God will guide you in the direction you need to go.

Real-girl Confession: "If I tell and my brother goes to jail, it will be my fault."

Indexed under: bullies, fear

Devotion #76

"[God] . . . is my refuge, a rock where no enemy can reach me."

(Psalm 62:7 NLT)

Wrong Turn!

Jacqui rode the city bus downtown every day after school to the building where her mom worked. There, she did homework in the lounge until Mom was ready to go home. Their apartment building wasn't in the safest area of town, and Mom didn't want Jacqui staying home alone. Jacqui didn't mind. She read on the bus, so the time went fast. One day, though, she was extra absorbed in her mystery. When she glanced up at the end of the chapter, Jacqui didn't recognize any of the buildings the bus was whizzing past. She had missed her stop!

She had to get off, but where was she? How far back was Mom's building? She had no more money to buy another ticket. Jacqui's heart pounded. *God, help me*, she prayed. *I'm so scared. Show me what to do!*

Jacqui looked around her. At some point, the bus had nearly filled up. The man across the aisle looked friendly enough, but she knew about the dangers of talking to strangers. What was it Jacqui's mom always said when she had a problem? "Go to the throne before going to the phone." She meant that she went to God's throne for help before going to the phone to call a friend for advice. Mom said God was her solid rock in times of trouble or problems.

The bus rolled along, block after block, while Jacqui prayed for help. According to her mom, God's answers sometimes came quickly. Other times it took a while. Jacqui breathed deeply, hoping this was one of God's "quickly" times.

Jacqui closed her eyes and waited for God to give her a good idea. *Tell the bus driver*, popped into her mind. So when the bus stopped for another passenger, Jacqui hurried to the driver and told him what had happened. "How can I get back to Mom's building?" she asked.

The driver handed Jacqui his cell phone. "Tell your mom you'll be twenty minutes late."

Jacqui called her mom and then rode the bus until it looped around and came back to the right stop. "Thank you!" Jacqui said to the driver as she got off the bus. *And thank you, God*, she added silently.

More to Explore: "The LORD is my rock, and my fortress, and my deliverer; my God, my strength, in whom I will trust." (Psalm 18:2 KJV)

Connecting to God: "Dear God, when I feel lost and don't know what to do, show me the next step to take. Help me to be calm while I wait for your answer. Amen."

Journal Prompt: When you are lost, does God know where you are? Could that answer help you? How?

Take Action: While finding her way home, Jacqui needed to stay safe. On the bus ride, a man sat down across the aisle. He seemed friendly, but he was still a stranger. How could Jacqui be polite, and yet stay safe? See the right and wrong responses below.

Man: "Whew! I nearly missed the bus! Hi, I'm John Black."

Jacqui: "Hi. I'm Jacqui Smith." [*Wrong!* Do not give your name to strangers.]

INSTEAD

Man: "Whew! I nearly missed the bus! Hi, I'm John Black."

Jacqui: "Good thing you made it," Jacqui said, and then turned to look out her window. [*Right!* Jacqui did not give her name in return, and her action was a polite message that she didn't want to talk to him.]

######

Man: "How about a sip of my soda?"

Jacqui: "No, thanks." [Good response. She draws a boundary, but is polite.]

Man: "Oh, come on," he said, smiling. "It's so hot out today." [Warning sign: he ignores your "no" to give you something, hoping you will feel like you owe him a favor in return.]

Jacqui: "Well, okay." [*Wrong* response!]

INSTEAD

Man: "How about a sip of my soda?"

Jacqui: "No, thanks." [Good response. She draws a boundary, but is polite.]

Man: "Oh, come on," he said, smiling. "It's so hot out today."

Jacqui: (firmly) "I said no." Jacqui moved several seats closer to the driver. [Jacqui ignores his pressure and puts distance between them. A wise move! *Right* response.]

Real-girl Confession: "When I finally found Dad at the state fair, I wanted to cry like a baby."

Indexed under: fear

Devotion #77

"We know that in all things God works for the good of those who love him, who have been called according to his purpose."

(Romans 8:28)

When Life is a Pain

Simone dug her house key from her pocket, then unlocked the front door. Her little sister, Marnie, dashed underneath her arm, knocking her sideways. Marnie ran for the TV and tuned in to her favorite after-school cartoon show.

"You stepped on me!" Simone shouted over the cartoon noise. "And pick up this stupid book bag!"

Marnie ignored her. Simone was tempted to throw her lunch bag and books across the living room. She resented having to come home after school to watch her little sister. Mom had taken a daytime job, so she wasn't at home when school let out.

Instead, Simone was home when she'd rather be at basketball practice with her friends. She missed walking home with her friends after practice. Now she had to babysit Marnie every day, do homework, and start supper. Life just wasn't fun anymore!

She knew it wasn't Mom's fault, but Simone resented her not being there anymore. Sighing, Simone read the note on the kitchen counter about what to cook for supper. Ugh. Another "frugal" recipe made with ground turkey.

Simone flipped on the radio station, then went to the fridge for the turkey, onions, and green peppers. Music filled the kitchen and Simone's mind, and she was glad not to think.

At four o'clock, the music stopped and a speaker came on. Simone recognized the voice of a lady preacher her mom listened to. Simone wanted to find another music station. Her hands were greasy from mixing the onions into the ground turkey, and she wiped them on a paper towel.

But as she reached for the radio, the speaker's words stopped Simone. "When God allows difficult things to happen in your life," the preacher said, "he promises to bring something good from them. Romans 8:28 says that 'in all things God works for the good of those who love him.' Not just in some things, but in *all* things. Not just in other people's things, but *your* things."

Simone leaned against the counter. Was that speaker talking about a kid's life too? Simone knew that she loved God and that she was a follower of Jesus. So according to that speaker, Romans 8:28 applied to her too.

The speaker continued, "God might not immediately change your circumstances. While waiting to see the good, you can either sink into discouragement or trust God to bring you through the hard time into a happier time. You can trust him for the outcome."

Simone was tired of being angry, so she decided to trust God to bring something good from her situation. It didn't happen overnight. But while fixing meals that year, Simone discovered that she loved baking, especially cakes. She took a free cake-decorating class at the YWCA, and soon she was making beautiful birthday cakes for friends. Simone even considered becoming a chef one day.

More to Explore: "That is why we never give up ... For our present troubles are small and won't last very long. Yet they produce for us a glory that ... will last forever!" (2 Corinthians 4:16 – 17 NLT)

Connecting to God: "Dear God, I really don't like what's happening in my life right now. Please turn things around. And give me patience while I wait for you to bring something good out of this situation. Amen."

Journal Prompt: Ask a tough question.

Take Action: Learn the Cooking Commandments!

1. *Be clean*: Wash your hands and make sure that all preparation areas are clean.
2. *Protect yourself*: Avoid loose sleeves that can catch on things. Tie long hair back. Use only dry, thick potholders and oven mitts.
3. *Be careful with water*: Wipe up spilled liquids. Keep electrical appliances away from water and wet hands.
4. *Use a knife carefully*: Keep knives visible, not hidden by a dishtowel or in soapy water.
5. *Don't spill the pot*: Keep pot and pan handles pointed to the center of the stove where they can't be bumped.

Real-girl Confession: "I just want to be a kid — not the mom!"

Indexed under: waiting on God

Devotion #78

"One who was there had been an invalid for thirty-eight years. When Jesus saw him lying there and learned that he had been in this condition for a long time, he asked him, 'Do you want to get well? . . . Get up! Pick up your mat and walk.'"

(John 5:5–6, 8)

"Are You Serious?"

Aliya was so depressed that she couldn't crawl out of bed. Her family had moved to a new apartment, and she had to change schools. Schoolwork had always been a struggle, but she'd always had her best friend, Molly, to help her and make her laugh. Aliya didn't think she could face one more day at her new school with the sea of strange faces.

Finally, she was hungry enough to drag herself out of bed. As she poured cereal into a bowl, she wondered how Mom managed to get up early every morning. But there she was, already at the kitchen table, reading her Bible.

Aliya plopped down opposite her. "Does that really help?" she asked, pointing at the Bible.

Mom looked up and smiled. "I couldn't make it through the day if I didn't meet with God first. You should try it."

Aliya shrugged. *Maybe I will sometime,* she thought, *but not today.* She was too depressed.

When her depression started getting worse, Aliya decided to join Mom at the kitchen table for her own early morning time with God. To Aliya's surprise, it really *did* help. She not only felt better, but she even found answers for her problems.

She discovered that as a believer, she could line her thoughts up with the Holy Spirit. She could *choose* to think about better things — things that made her feel positive and hopeful about school. Her thoughts were her choice.

Aliya noticed that frequently in the Bible when Jesus healed people, he told them to rise, pick up their bedrolls, and get moving. Jesus did the healing, but the people he healed also had to do something. She realized she needed to pray for God's help at school, but she also needed to do her part by studying harder and being friendlier at school.

Her life didn't change overnight, but Aliya didn't give up. She kept spending time with God, thinking good thoughts, and working hard. In time, she had plenty of friends — and she didn't feel depressed anymore.

More to Explore: "[Jesus] said to the paralyzed man, 'I tell you, get up, take your mat and go home.'" (Luke 5:24)

Connecting to God: "Dear Lord, sometimes I feel depressed about my life. Please, heal my sadness and help me do my part. Remind me to think right thoughts and do the things I can to make my life better. Amen."

Journal Prompt: Gratitude often helps chase away depression, so list ten things you're grateful to God for.

Take Action: Not all depression comes from thinking wrong thoughts. If spending time with God and changing your thoughts doesn't help your depression, it might be because your depression has a different basis. It can be caused by a medical reason or a big shock or trauma. If you feel depressed for a long time, tell someone you trust. Get help from a parent, teacher, counselor, pastor, or doctor.

Real-girl Confession: "I feel nervous all the time and have nightmares and cry for no reason."

Indexed under: depression, loneliness, thoughts

Devotion #79

"Let us strip off every weight that slows us down, especially the sin that so easily trips us up. And let us run with endurance the race God has set before us."

(Hebrews 12:1 NLT)

The Pit of Self-Pity

Leslie had a rough summer. She became sick and was hospitalized for three days. What the doctors told her was a shock. Her pancreas had stopped producing something called insulin. She had a disease called diabetes, and she would have to take medicine for the rest of her life. Every day, she would have to give herself insulin through a needle.

While in the hospital, Leslie learned how to give herself shots. The tiny needles didn't hurt too much, but she got tired of sticking herself several times a day. When she returned to school, she carried a medical kit with her. Before lunch, she'd disappear into the restroom to give herself a shot. Even though she was very careful about monitoring her insulin, sometimes she got sick.

One night at bedtime, Leslie dissolved into tears and buried her face in her pillow. She was still crying when a hand touched her back. She jerked her head up.

"It's just me," Mom said, handing her a tissue. "I thought I heard you crying. Do you feel sick?"

"Not really," Leslie mumbled, sniffling. Mom raised one eyebrow in question. Finally Leslie blurted out, "It's so unfair! None of my friends has some awful medical condition. Just me. Nobody else has to give herself shots and be so careful."

"Honey, I know that dealing with your diabetes is a big adjustment. It will take time. When you're exhausted or feeling sick, it's tempting to go overboard and feel sorry for yourself."

Leslie frowned. That wasn't a very nice thing to say to a sick person!

Her mom hugged her close. "Self-pity feels good at first, but it will actually drag you down even deeper into a pit of sad feelings. Like most pits, it's easier to stay away from the edge than to climb out after you've jumped in."

Leslie didn't like what Mom said about self-pity, but ... it *was* true that crying and carrying on made her feel even worse after a while.

"But how can I feel better about being sick?" Leslie asked.

"I've found that the easiest way to stop self-pity is to thank God for all the *good* things in your life. Yes, you might need insulin every day. So thank God for your legs and lungs and eyes that work just fine! If you list all the parts of your body that still work, you'll be amazed."

Leslie decided to give up feeling sorry for herself. She chose instead to be grateful for her doctors—and for the medicine that was keeping her alive. It was time to get on with living the life God had given her.

More to Explore: "We do this by keeping our eyes on Jesus, the champion who initiates and perfects our faith." (Hebrews 12:2 NLT)

Connecting to God: "Dear God, sometimes I get so tired of having problems, and I fall into the pit of self-pity. Remind me to keep my eyes on you and not give up. Help me to stop feeling sorry for myself and to be grateful for your loving care instead. Amen."

Journal Prompt: When life feels unfair, you might feel sorry for yourself. Is there a situation in your life that doesn't seem fair?

Take Action: Do you — or someone you love — have a medical condition you worry about? Here are some ways to handle it:

Get the facts. If you go to the Internet for information, ask an adult to search with you. The amount of information on the web can be overwhelming. An adult can find information that's written for kids.

Talk it out. Talking to someone — especially a trusted adult — can provide a source of support for you. A friend can give you a hug, or pray with you, or go for a walk with you.

Remember that God created the human body — and it's AMAZING! Sometimes things go wrong with a person's body. But it's good to think about how fabulous the body is and how God has made it very good at getting well. For many illnesses, the body heals itself without any special medicines or medical procedures.

Real-girl Confession: "I really worry when Dad gets sick. I don't want him to go to the hospital again."

Indexed under: health/health crisis, self-pity

Devotion #80

"Lead me in Your truth and teach me, for You are the God of my salvation; for You I wait all the day."

(Psalm 25:5 NASB)

Pray—Don't Jump!

Beth started gaining weight after the doctors said her mom had cancer. A year filled with operations and chemotherapy treatments had been rough for the whole family. Dad kept saying everything would be fine. And Beth found it easier not to worry if she let herself get distracted by the TV, especially if she also ate something sweet. Dad was often busy helping Mom, either at the hospital or at home, so Beth ate many of her meals alone.

Mom eventually got well. Her hair grew back in, and she went back to work. It was as if nothing had changed—except that Beth had gained twenty pounds. Her clothes were too tight, she couldn't run or dance like she used to, and she hated looking in the mirror. The only thing that made her feel better was eating sweets.

Finally, in desperation, Beth prayed and asked God to help her lose the weight. She wanted to look and feel better. After saying, "Amen," Beth threw away all her candy and chips. She decided to skip supper and jog several miles instead. God would help her get rid of that weight.

Instead of feeling better, Beth became sick after too many skipped meals and too many long exercise sessions. One day at school, she was so dizzy she couldn't participate in gym class. As she lay in the nurse's office, she prayed again. "God, I know I asked you to help me lose weight, but I didn't wait for you to show me what to do. I tried to fix the problem myself, but now I'm ready to listen to you."

As she gazed around the nurse's office, Beth's glance fell on the brightly colored nutrition charts on the wall. In simple words and pictures, it showed a healthful diet. Other charts showed how to have fun while getting fit.

Beth smiled. She hadn't expected God's answer to be immediate, but there was the writing on the wall. When the nurse came back, Beth had some questions for her about losing weight in a safe way.

More to Explore: "Be still before the Lord and wait patiently for him." (Psalm 37:7)

Connecting to God: "Dear God, sometimes I get impatient, and I forget to wait for your directions. I try to fix problems on my own and end up getting into more trouble. Help me listen to you and wait patiently for you to show me what to do. Amen."

Journal Prompt: While you wait for something to happen, what can you do with your anxious feelings?

Take Action: Have you ever run ahead of God? Maybe you prayed and asked him for help, but then immediately tried to fix the problem yourself. You didn't wait and give God a chance to direct you. It's hard to wait for God to answer prayer, but he has the best plan to solve your problem. Wait for him to show you what it is.

Real-girl Confession: "I feel like I'm *always* waiting for something to happen."

Indexed under: health/health crisis, waiting on God

Devotion #81

"Accept one another, then, just as Christ accepted you, in order to bring praise to God."

(Romans 15:7)

"It's Just Who I Am!"

Stepsisters Kate and Melissa were only a year apart, but they were worlds apart in their personalities. It might not have mattered so much, if they hadn't shared a bedroom.

"Mom, I can't stand it!" Kate protested, pacing back and forth. "There must be another place to put her besides my room."

"You know there isn't," Mom said. "Can't you work out your differences?"

"How? Look at this mess!" Kate cried. "She leaves things wherever she drops them. If I didn't clean up both sides of the room, it would look like a dump. I can't make her do her share." She threw her hands up in the air. "She's such a ditz! She can't even make a simple decision. Just ordering a pizza with her drives me nuts! I know what I want on my half." She snapped her fingers. "But Melissa? She thinks … and thinks … and thinks some more before choosing something. And then she says, 'Maybe I'll change that.'"

Mom smiled. "I know that can be irritating." She paused. "What does Melissa think about you?"

Kate shrugged. "She says I'm bossy and need to relax more."

Mom laughed out loud. "You're *both* right," she said. "You girls have very different God-given personalities. One isn't right and one wrong—God made you different. We *all* have personality strengths—and weaknesses."

Kate was furious. "You think it's all right for me to do all the cleaning while she sits around?"

"No, but yelling at her isn't right either."

Kate frowned and then nodded slowly. She realized her bossiness was only making things worse. "I guess I do need to lighten up a bit, but how? She's so irritating."

"Ask God to give you some ideas to make things better. He will."

That weekend Kate worked out a system with Melissa where they cleaned the room together each night while listening to music, and then finished with a bedtime snack. Kate even discovered some things she liked about her stepsister! She thanked God for helping them work through their differences and begin to appreciate each other.

More to Explore: "Create in me a pure heart, O God, and renew a steadfast spirit within me." (Psalm 51:10)

Connecting to God: "Dear God, thank you for making me the way you did. Help me to appreciate the positive side of my personality—and help me to appreciate personalities that are different than mine. Amen."

Journal Prompt: If you were trapped on an island with another person, what personality type would you find the hardest to be around?

Take Action: It's important to accept personalities that bug you. It's just as important to not be irritating yourself. Do you have any of these personality traits that cause friction? If so, ask God to help you eliminate these weaknesses.

Google Girl: the person who thinks she knows everything and is smarter than others

Super Talker: can't let the other person talk because she thinks her life story is so much more interesting than anything the other person might say

Attention Seeker: needs to have all eyes on her and will do whatever is necessary to get attention

Nosy Nellie: asks probing questions that go beyond interest in another person, asking for very personal facts that are none of her business

Rude Rita: cuts people off mid-sentence, brushes off others' opinions, ignores others who are talking

Real-girl Confession: "She makes these rude remarks and is driving me nuts!"

Indexed under: stepfamilies

Devotion #82

"We don't yet see things clearly. We're squinting in a fog, peering through a mist. But it won't be long before the weather clears and the sun shines bright! We'll see it all then, see it all as clearly as God sees us, knowing him directly just as he knows us!"

(1 Corinthians 13:12 MSG)

"I Don't Understand!"

Faith's family had been excited for months, ever since Mom's ultrasound had revealed that she was carrying a baby girl. They'd named her Juliana, and they'd fixed up the nursery across the hall from Faith's room.

Dad finally took Mom to the hospital Sunday afternoon while Grandma stayed with Faith. They played games and watched a movie, but Faith never strayed far from the phone. Finally, the call came at bedtime. They were stunned when they heard the news.

There had been a problem while Juliana was being born, and she couldn't breathe on her own. She was seven pounds, six ounces, and looked perfect in every way, but she'd been born dead. Faith's chest pounded, and she cried harder than she'd ever cried in her life.

"Why, Grandma?" she asked. "I'm so confused. Why did this happen?"

Later, at bedtime, Faith asked, "If God is good, and he can control everything, why did this terrible thing happen to our family?"

"It makes no sense at all," Grandma agreed, wiping her eyes. "Sometimes, there just aren't any answers that would satisfy us." She hugged Faith close. "Don't try to figure it out. You might not know why until you get to heaven. Trying too hard to understand now will just torment you."

"Then what do we do?" Faith asked. "It hurts so much."

"The Bible says to trust in the Lord with all your heart and not rely on your own understanding." She stroked Faith's hair. "If you do that, the Holy Spirit will give you peace that everything will be all right. God knows why this happened, and he's still in control. Just keep trusting him even though you don't understand. He loves you and is with you no matter what you go through."

Faith thought about Grandma's words. She still hurt deeply and had no answers to her questions, but she chose to trust that God loved them and would help them through this painful time.

More to Explore: "We walk by faith, not by sight." (2 Corinthians 5:7 NKJV)

Connecting to God: "Dear God, I don't understand at all why you let this terrible thing happen. But I know you love us, and I trust you. Thank you for being with us and helping us through this time. Amen."

Journal Prompt: Write about a favorite memory of a loved one who has passed on to heaven.

Take Action: After a loved one dies, you might feel many different things — and they're all normal stages of grief:

Physical symptoms (headaches, stomachaches, trouble sleeping)
Difficulty talking about feelings

Feeling helpless and hopeless

Anger; wanting to fight with people

Depression; sadness

Difficulty paying attention

Don't ignore these symptoms. Talk to a trusted adult about your feelings and journal about them.

Some experts say there are **five stages of grief**, but people don't always move through the stages in order. Not everyone experiencing a loss goes through each stage. But these common stages can help us identify what we may be feeling as we learn to live without the thing or person we have lost.

Stage 1: **Denial** (This stage is being in shock. We just can't—or won't—believe this awful thing has happened to us! We may feel numb.)

Stage 2: **Anger** (The shock has worn off, and we are angry at everyone: the person who died, God, and ourselves. We hate that this has happened to us!)

Stage 3: **Bargaining** (We think "If only ..." and "What if ..." We search desperately for a way to turn back the clock so we don't have to feel the loss.)

Stage 4: **Sadness** (The tears, the depression, and the agony feel like it will go on forever. This is the stage where you do the most crying. Let yourself feel it and cry as much as you need to.)

Stage 5: **Acceptance** (This is not necessarily a happy stage, but it is calmer, and we aren't fighting the reality of what has happened anymore. We begin to look ahead and create a life without the person or thing we have lost.)

Real-girl Confession: "How long does it take to stop hurting?"

Indexed under: confusion, crisis, death

Devotion #83

"God blesses those who patiently endure testing."

(James 1:12 NLT)

Accidents and Attitudes

Felicia had a bike accident the week before school started—and broke her collarbone. She bit back tears when she was lifted into the ambulance. She was brave when the nurse scrubbed her bloody elbow and hand. When the doctor set the broken bone in place and strapped on her back brace, she gasped but didn't cry out.

The first day at home wasn't too bad. Three friends visited her, and two even brought gifts. Felicia hated the back brace though. It rubbed her skin sore, and no matter what shirt she wore, the big straps showed.

"I'll still be wearing this ugly thing when school pictures are taken!" she told Mom. Even worse, she couldn't ride her bike till the brace came off. Six whole weeks! Mom would have to drop her off at school like she was a little first-grader. "Why did this happen to *me?*" Felicia whined.

"Life happens to everyone, Felicia," her older sister, Kaila, said. "Complaining won't help. In fact, it will just make you feel *worse.*"

"Well, I'm not wearing this ugly brace at school," Felicia said

258

through gritted teeth. "I'll leave it in my locker. Mom will never know."

Steph sat beside her on the bed. "Be patient, Felicia. Stay busy, and before you know it, the collarbone will be healed." She raised one eyebrow. "But it won't heal right if you don't wear the brace the whole six weeks. The bone will reconnect crooked and stick out instead. You want a huge bump there for the rest of your life?"

Felicia sighed. "No." She glanced at her scraped arm. At least it was her left arm. "I guess I'll need to do something different for a while to stay busy."

Kaila took her hand. "Let's pray about it. 'Lord, please help Felicia to be patient while she heals. And show her things she still can do while she waits. Amen.'"

Felicia sat up straighter. "I guess I'll wear this thing after all," she said. "You know, I never did finish that huge dolphin puzzle to hang on my wall. I can work on that."

"Want me to take you to the library?" Kaila asked. "We can get some funny books and comedies to watch on DVD."

Felicia smiled. "Are you saying my sense of humor needs help?"

"Laughter *is* the best medicine." Kaila grinned. "Let's go!"

More to Explore: "After [Abraham] had patiently endured, he obtained the promise." (Hebrews 6:15 NKJV)

Connecting to God: "Dear God, some problems seem to drag on forever. When I can't see the end, I get impatient and complain. Help me to have a patient attitude and trust you one day at a time without grumbling or complaining. Amen."

Journal Prompt: When you are recovering from an illness or injury, what is the hardest thing that tries your patience?

Take Action: Positive ways to stay busy and keep your mind off your pain include...

Listen to books on CD, free from the library. Sometimes it's easier to listen to a book than to read.

Play classic board games, such as Monopoly or Scrabble.

Rent a movie or a whole season of a TV series. Most libraries have them to check out for free or a small fee.

Read the original magical book series, *The Chronicles of Narnia* by C.S. Lewis

Do crossword puzzles or Sudoku puzzles.

Connect with an old friend or a relative you've lost touch with. Try sending him or her a card or letter through old-fashioned mail.

Become an expert on a specific subject of interest — rent documentaries, read books, and do online research on a certain subject or hobby.

Don't let it all be about you. Make cards for people you know who are sick or have been housebound themselves for a long time. Also make thank-you cards for people who sent gifts, cards, flowers, or visited. Thinking of others is a good way to make sure the attitude is healthy while the body is healing.

Real-girl Confession: "Feeling good again is better than almost anything!"

Indexed under: complaining, health/health crisis

Devotion #84

"Readily adjust yourself to [people, things] and give yourselves to humble tasks."

(Romans 12:16 AMP)

An Attitude Adjustment

Lupe knew her grandfather's health was failing. Sometimes, he forgot to take his medication, and twice he fell and sprained his ankle. She wanted to help Grandpa, but she hadn't counted on giving up her bedroom for him.

"There's no other choice, Lupe," Mom said. "You'll need to share a bedroom with Sylvia so Grandpa can have your room. He doesn't need a nursing home yet, but he can't live alone anymore either. I'm sorry about your room, but you'll have to adjust."

Lupe loved her grandfather, and she'd enjoy having him live with her family. But her teenage sister was sloppy, she was up all hours, and her music was always deafening. Lupe loved having her own room, where she could shut the door and read in peace and quiet. Now she would have no privacy at all!

Lupe was sitting on the front step when her father came home. "You look glum," he said, sitting down beside her. "What's up?"

"I'm adjusting," Lupe muttered.

"Oh." Dad hugged her shoulders. "Mom told you about Grandpa moving in then?"

Lupe nodded. "I really love Grandpa. I do, but ..."

"I know," Dad said. "It's still hard to adjust to circumstances we can't change."

"And *people* we can't change!" Lupe cried, thinking of her sister's noise.

Dad patted her knee. "It's normal to feel angry and shocked and sad when you get a surprise you don't want," Dad said, "but that's life, Lupe. Unexpected events happen to everyone. God will help you adjust and change your thinking if you ask him."

That evening after supper, Lupe took a very long walk to pray about her situation. She finally decided that if she didn't adjust, she'd have no peace or joy. She had no choice about moving in with Sylvia. They could be upset with each other for months—or try to find positive things about rooming together.

Heading home, Lupe chose to search for some *good* things about her situation. *It might even be fun!* she thought.

More to Explore: "Let us be of the same mind." (Philippians 3:16 NKJV)

Connecting to God: "Dear God, I am so upset about what's happening, but I can't change it. Help me accept this change and adjust my attitude so I can be at peace about it. Amen."

Journal Prompt: How can you change your negative thoughts about a difficult situation?

Take Action: Are you sharing a room with a sibling? Try these tips to get along...

Lights out: Find a middle ground. If one girl has lights out at 10:00 p.m., the other at 8:00 p.m., meet in the middle at 9:00 p.m.

Quiet time: Choose specific times where no one watches TV, listens to music without earphones, or talks on the phone.

Private space: Divide the room with area rugs so each girl has her own "territory."

Organizing: Give each girl a set of bookshelves, some plastic bins, or colored laundry baskets that fit under the bed, and if possible, a table or desk.

Real-girl Confession: "I love my sis, but she's driving me *crazy!*"

Indexed under: change

Devotion #85

"I want women to be modest in their appearance. They should wear decent and appropriate clothing."

(1 Timothy 2:9 NLT)

Taken by Surprise

Sage went tent camping with her cousin Josie's family at a nearby lake. She loved cooking over an open fire, sleeping in a sleeping bag, and swimming in the lake.

One afternoon, when Sage went into their big tent to get her swim fins, her uncle followed her inside. "Ready to go swimming?" he asked. "It's getting pretty hot."

Sage grinned and waved the fins at him. "I'm going to win the race with Josie this time," she said. "These are my secret weapon!"

Her uncle laughed, and then turned and zipped the tent door closed. Sage frowned, feeling uncomfortable, but not knowing why exactly.

"I'm going back outside now," Sage said, edging past her uncle to the door.

"Aren't you going to change into your bathing suit?" he asked. "You can't swim in jeans." He took off his shirt. "I'm getting my swimming trunks on now too."

Sage froze, not knowing what to do. He was her uncle, and she loved him, but this didn't feel right. She didn't want to seem rude or ungrateful, but his suggestion sounded wrong. She'd had more than one talk with her mom about girls needing to dress modestly, like the Bible taught. She knew she was supposed to wear decent clothing that covered her appropriately at all times. And she sure didn't want to see her uncle naked either!

Her uncle kicked off his shoes and peeled off his socks. "Come on. I'll race you to see who gets changed faster." He stopped and smiled. "It's all right. You don't need to be embarrassed. I've seen girls before." He stepped closer. "Need some help with those buttons in back?"

"No!" Sage said firmly. "I'll change later with Josie." With shaking fingers she unzipped the tent door and slipped outside, forgetting her swim fins.

For the rest of the weekend, she didn't go anywhere at all without Josie. After she got home from the weekend trip, she told her parents about it. It was hard to talk about—and it was difficult for her parents to hear—but she knew they would want to know about it right away.

More to Explore: "Don't let anyone think less of you because you are young. Be an example to all believers . . . in the way you live." (1 Timothy 4:12 NLT)

Connecting to God: "Dear God, something scary happened to me, and I feel kind of sick to my stomach about it. Help me to be strong and say no loud and clear when someone wants me to do something I know is wrong. Amen."

Journal Prompt: Some people say it's *your* fault when *they* do a bad thing. Whose fault is it really? Why do you think so?

Take Action: You are playing at a friend's house, and her older brother wants to take pictures of you without any clothes on. You like your friend a lot, but the brother's request makes you very uncomfortable. What do you do?

1. Say you don't want to have your picture taken at all.
2. Agree to do it if your friend goes first.
3. Leave and go home immediately.
4. Tell her brother you'll think about it.
5. Tell your parents what happened as soon as you get home.
6. Numbers 4 and 5
7. Numbers 1, 3, and 5

Real-girl Confession: "He blamed *me* for what *he* did!"

Indexed under: abuse/sexual, honesty

Devotion #86

"Take my yoke upon you and learn from me, for I am gentle and humble in heart, and you will find rest for your souls. For my yoke is easy and my burden is light."

(Matthew 11: 29–30)

Trading Yokes

"I don't know what I'd do without you, Nita," Mom often said. "You're such a help to me. You're my right-hand man."

That always made Nita feel good, at least for a while. It helped her keep going when worries overwhelmed her. In their single-parent home, there was barely enough money. Nita worried when she noticed bills marked "overdue" in big red letters. Would they end up living under a bridge or in a homeless shelter?

Nita did homework and fixed supper before Mom got home. Her older brother, Nick, took off with friends instead and rarely did his homework. Nita worried about him too. Some of his new friends were so creepy. And for guys with no jobs, they sure had a lot of money to spend.

One night, she tossed and turned in bed until midnight. Wearily, Nita went to the bathroom for a drink of water.

"You still awake?" Mom asked as she passed by in the hall. "How come?"

"No reason," Nita said, hoping her smile didn't look phony. "Just a lot on my mind."

Mom moved behind Nita and gave her a neck rub. "I was just getting ready to make some hot chocolate. Want some?"

"With marshmallows?" Nita asked, her smile real this time.

"You bet. As many as you want."

A few minutes later they were sitting at the kitchen table. Nita scooped up the melted marshmallows and licked her spoon. "Isn't Nick in yet?" she asked.

"No. He's nearly an hour late, and he's not answering his phone," Mom said. "I'm sure he's fine though."

Nita wasn't sure at all, but Mom hadn't seen his new friends. Nick always managed to be gone before Mom got home from work. Nita didn't know what to do, not about Nick, and not about their unpaid bills.

"Want to tell me why you can't sleep?" Mom asked. "You look exhausted, if you don't mind me saying so."

Tears welled up in Nita's eyes, but she brushed them away. "I am."

"It's okay, you know," Mom said. "Even right-hand men get tired."

Nita nodded. At first it was hard to talk, but then the words poured out. She finally told her mom about the worries keeping her awake at night.

"No wonder you're exhausted," Mom said. "You're feeling responsible for things you don't have any control over. The pressure of being the head of a household is too much for you. That's not your job — it's mine." She squeezed Nita's hand. "God will give me the strength to deal with finances and Nick's behavior. But the load's too heavy for you, honey."

Nita nodded in agreement.

"Let's trade yokes, okay?" Mom asked.

"What's that mean?"

Mom drew a figure on her paper napkin. "See this wooden

yoke? It fits over a person's shoulders for carrying buckets, one at each end. A yoke helps a person do work, but you can't carry loads beyond your strength. Your knees would buckle."

"Is that what I'm doing?" Nita asked.

"Yes, sometimes, when you worry about *my* responsibilities. God never intended for you to do that. Instead, Jesus invites believers to put on *his* yoke. These are our true responsibilities. If we do that, Jesus helps us carry the load. He promises his yoke is easy and his burden is light."

Mom helped Nita see which things she was truly responsible for—her homework and cooking supper. Nita stopped worrying about Mom's responsibilities and prayed for Mom instead.

More to Explore: "Is not this the kind of fasting I have chosen: to untie the cords of the yoke, to set the oppressed free and break every yoke?" (Isaiah 58:6)

Connecting to God: "Dear God, I'm afraid of many things I can't control. Help me to see the things that are my responsibility and trust you to take care of everything else. Amen."

Journal Prompt: Are you carrying a load of trouble that belongs to someone else?

Take Action: Three things to do with burdens, or troubles, that weigh you down:

1. Some burdens are to be *shouldered* by you. (Galatians 6:4 – 5)
2. Some burdens are to be *shared* with others. (Galatians 6:1 – 2)
3. Some burdens should be *shifted* over to the Lord. (Psalm 55:22)

Real-girl Confession: "I don't have a clue what to do!"

Indexed under: finances, overloaded

Devotion #87

"O LORD my God, in You I put my trust."

(Psalms 7:1 NKJV)

"I Hate Surprises!"

Lilly didn't like surprises. She didn't like parties or deep water—or anything she couldn't control.

"I want to know everything before it happens," Lilly told her friend as they walked home from church. "I hate surprises!"

"Why?" Jaclyn asked. "Surprises are fun!"

Lilly shrugged. *Fun?* she thought. *No way!*

To Lilly, surprises meant things like fixing picnic food and waiting in the car, then hearing Dad yell, "Get out. We're not going." *Surprise!* It meant saving her money for a bike, but having the cash disappear. *Surprise!* It meant coming home from school to discover that Dad had packed up and left. *Surprise!*

No, as far as Lilly was concerned, she never wanted another surprise in her life.

Jaclyn studied her friend. "Why don't you like to be surprised?" she asked softly.

Tears welled up in Lilly's eyes, and she brushed them away in embarrassment. "Surprises are never good," she said. "I want to be prepared instead of taken by surprise."

"But *why?*"

"How else can I be ready and know what to do?" Lilly's voice was barely above a whisper. "Most surprises come from people not keeping promises."

"You mean your dad, don't you?" Jaclyn draped an arm over Lilly's shoulders. "No wonder you don't like to be surprised."

Lilly shuffled through the fallen leaves for several minutes, and then blurted out, "I don't really trust God either," she admitted. "I wish I could, but what if he's like other people in my life? I can't trust my real dad, so how can I trust my Father in heaven? Aren't fathers all alike?"

"No, they aren't," Jaclyn said. "Many fathers are like my dad, people you can trust who are kind and protect their families. I know that not all fathers break promises."

"That's what Mom says too." She held her Bible close. "She says I need to learn to trust my heavenly Father to be our provider and protector."

Jaclyn nodded. "Just remember that God is loving you all the time."

"I'll try." It wasn't easy, and it took some time. But slowly, by praying and reading God's promises in her Bible, Lilly began to trust God to take care of her. She couldn't always count on people to keep their promises, but she grew to understand that her heavenly Father would never let her down.

More to Explore: "God's way is perfect. All the LORD's promises prove true. He is a shield for all who look to him for protection." (Psalm 18:30 NLT)

Connecting to God: "Dear God, I get afraid when I don't know what is going to happen in my life. People don't always keep their promises. Help me trust you more and more as my heavenly Father. Remind me that I can always count on you because you never break your promises. Amen."

Journal Prompt: What are your favorite memories about an absent parent or relative?

Take Action: If your parents have chosen to divorce, you might have many questions. Here are some true statements...

"It's not your fault *at all* if your parent left."

"Getting help for problems is good."

"Jesus will always be with you. *Always.*"

"God will help you through this tough time and teach you important things."

Real-girl Confession: "People who make up stuff are hard to trust."

Indexed under: change, divorce, worry

Devotion #88

"Control your temper, for anger labels you a fool."

(Ecclesiastes 7:9 NLT)

Ready to Explode

Toni stomped around the house Saturday morning, kicking the chairs and hitting the table with her broom. She hated house-cleaning and washing dishes and babysitting her little sister. Every Saturday was the same. While Mom worked at a department store, Toni ran the house. It had been that way ever since Dad took a sales job and had to be gone so much. Mom needed to work more hours, so Toni needed to do Mom's job.

"This is so unfair!" she cried. That morning, her friends had gone roller-skating for another girl's birthday party. Toni couldn't go. Sometimes she was so angry, she felt like exploding.

"Toni?" her little sister screamed. "Come here! The toilet's overflowing!"

Toni took off running. "Wait until I get my hands on you, Renee! Don't you think I have enough to do without you making a stinkin' mess for me to clean up? What did you try to flush this time?"

Halfway through mopping the bathroom floor, the doorbell rang. "I don't believe it!" Toni cried.

"I'll get it," Renee said, jumping up.

Toni grabbed Renee's arm. "Oh, no, you don't."

"Ow! You're hurting me!"

"Then stop trying to pull loose. You can't answer the door." Toni put the mop down. "I need to look through the peephole first and see who it is."

She squinted and looked. It was Grandma. Toni sighed. Why couldn't Grandma show up when things were going right? Toni pasted a smile on her face and opened the door.

"Hi, Grandma—"

"The toilet flooded!" Renee cried. "And icky water got the hall carpet wet."

"Oh, dear," Grandma said. "Can I help?"

"Not really." Toni clenched her teeth in anger. "I feel like screaming or breaking Renee's neck. Or running away!"

"Sounds like you have your hands full," Grandma said, rolling up her sleeves. "Let's see what we can do." In half an hour, Toni and Grandma had mopped up the mess and sanitized the floor.

Out in the living room, Renee climbed into Grandma's lap and snuggled. Toni collapsed on the floor, resting her head on her folded arms. She took a deep breath, embarrassed at her outburst earlier. "Sorry about what I said before. I'm usually real calm."

"It's okay," Grandma said. "Feelings aren't wrong or bad. It isn't wrong to feel angry."

"Yes, it is!" Renee said. "Toni isn't supposed to grab my arm!"

"*Feelings* aren't wrong," Grandma repeated, "but what you *do* when you're angry might be wrong. Ask God to help you so your feelings don't control you. He will help you stay calm if you ask him."

"I pray, believe it or not," Toni said. "I just wish I didn't feel mad all the time, but I do."

"If that's the case," Grandma said, "God might be using your anger to tell you something's wrong. What's really bothering you?"

Toni hesitated, then she opened up and told Grandma how much she missed getting to do things with her friends. That night, Toni decided to tell Mom how she felt about missing the fun times on Saturdays. She was respectful, but she was also totally honest about how she felt.

After thinking about it, Mom worked out a schedule so Toni could be with her friends part of every Saturday, without any adult responsibilities.

More to Explore: "Everyone should be quick to listen, slow to speak and slow to become angry, because human anger does not produce the righteousness that God desires." (James 1:19 – 20)

Connecting to God: "Dear God, sometimes I get so mad about things happening in my life that I want to scream! Show me how to handle my anger the right way. Instead of blowing up at everyone, help me share how I feel with honesty and kindness. Amen."

Journal Prompt: What's the difference between something that makes you mad for just a minute and something that makes you stay angry for days or weeks?

Take Action: Some negative feelings are gifts from God for a good purpose.

If you never felt angry, you might do nothing about people or animals being mistreated.

If you never felt fear, you might cross the street in front of an oncoming car.

If you never felt lonely or unhappy, you might not try to make friends.

If you never felt worried, you might not pray for God's help.

Real-girl Confession: "I feel like screaming or breaking something."

Indexed under: anger, friendship, overloaded

Devotion #89

"May God, who gives this patience and encouragement, help you live in complete harmony with each other."

(Romans 15:5 NLT)

"I Want It Now!"

Peyton hated when Dad and Shawn fought. Shawn always wanted to do things, but Dad always thought he was too young. Peyton heard another fight erupt downstairs. At sixteen, Shawn had a new driver's license and expected Dad to give him the family car every weekend.

Their angry voices carried clear up to Peyton's bedroom.

"Why can't I take the car? The rodeo's only thirty miles away!"

"Stop yelling, and I'll tell you," Dad said.

Peyton knew from past arguments what Dad was going to say: Shawn was a brand-new driver, the highways at night were crowded, the rodeo got out late, and there were bound to be drunk drivers on the road home. As Dad had said before, Shawn needed more practice driving before he could safely drive out of town with his friends.

Peyton couldn't drive yet — and she didn't want to — but there were other things she wanted to do. Her friends were wearing dangly earrings and went to concerts at the stadium. Peyton wished she could too, but Dad said, "Not yet."

Mostly, though, she wanted the fights in her home to stop.

She prayed for that every night. Shawn often threatened to run away, and Peyton worried that he might do it.

The fighting didn't stop overnight. It didn't even stop in a month. But Peyton kept praying and didn't give up. She hoped that Shawn would learn to be patient and wait for Dad's timing—and God's. She knew she needed to learn the same lesson, but waiting was *hard*.

One night when Shawn woke her up slamming a door, Peyton stayed still and listened. Was that his bedroom door? Or had he finally decided to run away and slammed the front door on his way out? She lay in the dark and prayed.

Her bedroom door opened then, and a narrow stream of light shone across her bed from the hallway. Peyton sat up and saw Dad peeking in. "Just making sure you're okay," he whispered.

"I heard a door slam, and it woke me up," Peyton said. "Did Shawn leave?"

"No, he went to bed. Mad, but he went to bed." Dad sighed. "I'm sorry about the noise." He came in and sat on the side of her bed. "Shawn's in a big hurry to be an adult."

"I pray for him," Peyton said.

"Good. I do too." Dad patted her arm. "Keep praying. Sometimes when we pray, we get what we want right away. At other times, we wonder if our prayers will ever get answered."

"Like with Shawn?"

"Like many things," Dad said. "We need to keep remembering Psalm 37:4 that says, "Take delight in the Lord, and he will give you the desires of your heart."

"I don't understand," Peyton said.

"Well, it means that if you find your happiness in pleasing God and spending time with him, he will do one of two things. He might give you what you want—in his perfect timing. Or he will change your heart so that you actually want something different."

"So either way, it's a good answer, right?" Peyton asked.

"Exactly." Dad bent over and kissed her good-night. "Some answers seem to take a long time. We usually have some important lesson to learn first. So never give up!"

More to Explore: "The testing of your faith produces patience. But let patience have its perfect work, that you may be perfect and complete, lacking nothing." (James 1:3 – 4 NKJV)

Connecting to God: "Dear God, I get so frustrated waiting until I'm old enough to do the things I want to do. Teach me to trust your plan for me and remember that your timing is perfect. Help me to wait patiently for the things I want. Help me to want what *you* want! Amen."

Journal Prompt: What are some good ways to stay busy to make waiting seem to go faster?

Take Action: Two Ways to Wait

> *Passively*: A passive person hopes something good will happen and sits around waiting to see if it does. After a short time, she gives up because "nothing's happened." This is *not* what the Bible means by "waiting."
>
> *Eagerly*: This person waits with hope, believing the answer could arrive any minute. She knows every day that her problem could be solved that very day. She doesn't give up.

Real-girl Confession: "I'll explode if I have to wait any longer!"

Indexed under: rebellion, waiting on God

Devotion #90

"The Holy Spirit produces this kind of fruit in our lives: love, joy, peace, patience, kindness, goodness, faithfulness, gentleness, and self-control."

(Galatians 5:22–23 NLT)

Jealousy Attack!

Celeste loved seeing Dad every other weekend at his new house. She just wished she could be with him alone, without all those *other* people. There was his new wife, Janis, her five-year-old daughter, and now a baby boy. Her stepfamily was nice enough, but Celeste felt jealous of them. Very jealous! She was jealous of the time they spent with *her* dad. And she was jealous of their beautiful home because she and Mom had to live in a dinky duplex.

Celeste had honestly tried hard to like her stepfamily. The baby was cute, the little stepsister was very friendly, and Janis always acted glad to see Celeste. Even so, Celeste was quiet during her visits. She didn't want to be a part of *this* new family. She wanted her old family back together. She didn't feel any love for these people, no matter how much Dad wanted her to.

When she went home that weekend, she tried to tell her mom how she felt. But Mom exploded. "Of course you don't like his new family! Why would you even try? They don't deserve that new house or anything else!"

Celeste clammed up and went outside to the backyard. She weeded in their tiny vegetable garden, even though it didn't really need it. But *she* needed time alone to think.

"How was your weekend?" asked a voice above her head.

Celeste looked up, shading her eyes from the sun's glare. Standing over her was Nevaeh, the teenager from next door. "Hi, Nevaeh." She yanked another weed from the row of green beans. "It's a relief to come home. I don't fit in over there."

Nevaeh squatted down beside her. "I remember when I felt that way," she said. "My dad remarried eight years ago. It took four or five years before I fit in or any of them felt like my family."

Celeste's heart sank. "I can't stand it that long."

Nevaeh laughed. "I didn't think I could either. Thankfully, I didn't have to do it alone."

"Who helped you?" Celeste asked, recalling her mom's reaction earlier.

"God helped me. Believe me, by ourselves, none of us can show love — or patience or gentleness — to others. But if you're a follower of Jesus, you know the Holy Spirit lives inside you. *He* produces God's love in us, so we can pass it on to others."

"Would God do that for me too?" Celeste asked, feeling a flicker of hope.

"Oh, yes!" Neveah told her about Jesus rising from the dead for her sins and explained how to turn her life over to God. "Spend lots of time talking to God, and I'll get you a Bible to read. His love will fill you and eventually spill over onto others."

Celeste began doing that every day, and in time, she grew to really care for her stepfamily.

More to Explore: "Remain in me, and I will remain in you. For a branch cannot produce fruit if it is severed from the vine, and you cannot be fruitful unless you remain in me." (John 15:4 NLT)

Connecting to God: "Dear God, I just can't love certain people or be patient with them. Please grow the fruit of the Spirit in my heart so that I can love other people the way you do. Amen."

Journal Prompt: What keeps you stuck thinking about a past hurtful event so you can't enjoy good things in the present?

Take Action: On weekend visits, it can be tough living out of a suitcase and feeling like it's not really your home. Here are some ideas to make it seem more like home . . .

Ask if you can put up a poster or two.

Keep some of your things there, like a trophy or something you made at school.

Ask if you can have a cupboard or even a drawer you can keep things in.

Keep a toothbrush and a few spare clothes there.

Can you invite a friend over?

Can you give out the phone number so your best friend can call you?

(NOTE: If you're in a stepfamily like Celeste's, the "blending" process can take up to five years. Give it time. Give your stepfamily a chance.)

Real-girl Confession: "I know Dad's trying, but I don't fit in with his new family."

Indexed under: jealousy, salvation, stepfamilies

Resources

Alcohol Abuse

http://al-anon.alateen.org/for-alateen/how-will-alateen-help-me

Alateen is part of Al-Anon Family Groups. Alateen is a fellowship of young Al-Anon members, usually teenagers, whose lives have been affected by someone else's drinking. Alateen groups are sponsored by Al-Anon members who help the group to stay on track. Alateens come together to:

- share experiences, strength, and hope with each other
- discuss difficulties
- learn effective ways to cope with problems
- encourage one another
- help each other understand the principles of the Al-Anon program

Child Abuse

ChildHelp National Child Abuse Hotline

http://www.childhelp.org/pages/hotline-home

The Childhelp National Child Abuse Hotline 1-800-4-A-CHILD (1-800-422-4453) is dedicated to the prevention of child abuse. Serving the United States, its territories, and Canada, the Hotline is staffed 24 hours a day, 7 days a week with professional crisis counselors who, through interpreters, can provide assistance in 170 languages. The Hotline offers crisis intervention, information, literature, and referrals to thousands of emergency, social service, and support resources. All calls are anonymous and confidential.

Suicide

National Suicide Hotlines USA Toll-Free / 24 hours a day / 7 days a week

1-800-SUICIDE

1-800-784-2433

1-800-273-TALK

1-800-273-8255

1-800-799-4TTY (4889) Deaf Hotline

Also check the FRONT of the phone book for:
- suicide prevention
- crisis intervention
- hotlines — crisis or suicide
- community crisis center
- county mental health center
- hospital mental health clinic

Or call 911 and ask for help.

Drug Abuse Help

Drug Abuse Help Lines

Overcoming drug addiction and co-occurring disorders can seem impossible, but it's not. Expert help is available to ensure you or a loved one gain control and do a complete 180 degree turn towards the positive aspects of life.

Call 1-866-643-6144 to begin the process of change. A free, 24-hour-a-day, 7-days-per-week drug helpline is here to assist you. See also:

Drug Abuse Helpline: 800-234-8334

http://drugabusehelpline.net/

Domestic Violence Help

National Domestic Violence Hotline: 800-799-SAFE/800-799-7233 and 800-787-3224 (TTY).

24-hour-a-day hotline, provides crisis intervention and referrals to local services and shelters for victims of domestic abuse. English and Spanish speaking advocates are available 24 hours a day, seven days a week. Staffed by trained volunteers who are ready to connect people with emergency help in their own communities, including emergency services and shelters.

Runaways

National Runaway Switchboard: 800-621-4000

Provides crisis intervention and travel assistance to runaways. Provides information and local referrals to adolescents and families. Gives referrals to shelters nationwide. Also relays messages to, or sets up conference calls with, parents at the request of the child. Operates 24 hours a day, seven days a week.

CONFIDENTIAL Runaway Hotline: 800-231-6946

Stranger Danger

http://www.safetycops.com/stranger_danger.htm

http://www.kidpower.org/blog/kidnapping-prevention-checklist-for-parents

Internet Safety

http://www.netsmartz.org/internetsafety

Sources

Proverbs and quotations

http://quotationsbook.com/quote/38424/#sthash.BVYN4NWA.dpbs

Your Life, Your Voice (girls' issues)

http://www.yourlifeyourvoice.org

Four Spiritual Laws

http://www.campuscrusade.com/fourlawseng.htm

Death, Dying, Grief

http://www.recover-from-grief.com/grieving-children.html

http://childparenting.about.com/cs/emotionalhealth/a/childgrief.htm

http://www.nasponline.org/resources/crisis_safety/griefwar.pdf

http://www.fredrogers.org/new-site/par-death.html

Handling Change

http://jillkuzma.files.wordpress.com/2012/02/a-kids-guide-for-change.pdf

http://life.familyeducation.com/personal-finance/family/47247.html

Step Siblings Getting Along

http://www.cyh.com/HealthTopics/HealthTopicDetails.aspx?p=240&np=296&id=2089

Physical Abuse

http://www.crcvc.ca/docs/child_abuse.pdf

http://www.healthyplace.com/abuse/child-physical-abuse/healing-from-child-physical-abuse/

Money

http://themint.org/kids/saving-tricks.html

https://www.childwelfare.gov/pubs/factsheets/signs.cfm

Forgiving Yourself

http://www.huffingtonpost.com/rick-hanson-phd/forgive-yourself_b_906769.html

Worry

http://kidshealth.org/kid/feeling/thought/poll_worry.html

http://www.foxnews.com/health/2012/04/04/warning-your-child-may-worry-too-much/#ixzz2CITz0tuZ

Internet Safety

http://kidshealth.org/parent/positive/family/net_safety.html

http://www.fbi.gov/stats-services/publications/parent-guide

Topical Index